off a finger—or do worse. One recent theory about the death of Amelia Earhart is that she crashed her plane on a small atoll in the South Pacific and survived, but was gravely wounded and unable to fend off scavenging coconut crabs, who ate her…possibly alive.

The killer squirrel story we included in this volume is far less plausible. The "squirrels" are actually Australian sugar gliders, popular pets Down Under and elsewhere. They can nip and live in groups in the wild. But it's unlikely that even a huge mob of pissed-off sugar gliders would pose a real threat to humans.

Traveling Incognito: Pseudonyms in MAMs were as common as man-eating beasts. This gruesome rat-attack tale from the July 1973 *Male* was written by Walter Kaylin, but credited to "Ben Lewinson as told to Roland Empey." Empey was one of Kaylin's frequent pseuds, while Lewinson is the name of the story's fictional protagonist. Adding to the intrigue, the squirm-inducing illustration was provided by "Emmett Kaye"—a pseudonym of pantheon MAM artist Mort Künstler!

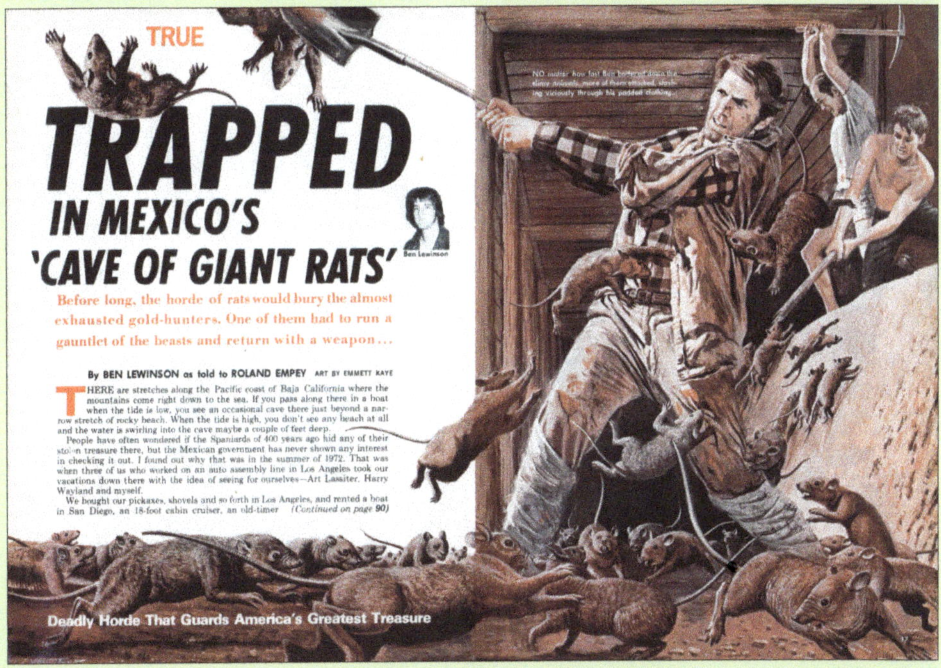

Male July 1973, art by Mort Künstler (as Emmett Kaye)

The third story in this book, "Terror Safari," comes from a short-lived men's adventure magazine with the hormone-infused title *Rage*. It's about a "lust-crazed gorilla" who kidnaps human women.

Of course, that old trope has long been played for laughs in comedy films. But as you'll see, the story is not designed to be humorous, even though the cover painting that illustrates it, by artist John Duillo, portrays a totally gonzo, gravity-defying scene.

The last two stories in this volume come from *Male*, one of the best and longest lasting men's adventure magazines. *Male* was one of the "Diamond Group" MAMs published by Magazine Management. Those magazines were a training ground for many writers who went on to international fame, such as Mario Puzo, Bruce Jay Friedman and Martin Cruz Smith—as well as for many others who, though less well known, earned a good living as professional writers.

Two of those pros were writers I knew: Robert F. Dorr, whose war and adventure stories we showcased in the book *A Handful of Hell*, and Walter Kaylin, whose over-the-top yarns are featured in our *He-Men, Bag Men, & Nymphos* collection. Bob passed away in 2016; Walter in 2017. We're proud to continue keeping their legacy in print.

I hope you enjoy this installment of *The Men's Adventure Library Journal* as much as we enjoyed putting it together. More are coming. ●

"The Moose Went Mad!"
Man's Magazine
March 1956
art by Frank Cozzarelli

THE MEN'S ADVENTURE LIBRARY JOURNAL

I WATCHED THEM Eat Me Alive

Killer Creatures in Men's Adventure Magazines

MensPulpMags.com   # new texture

The Men's Adventure Library Journal: I Watched Them Eat Me Alive is a New Texture publication. ISBN 978-1-943444-26-7 Covers and scans are reproduced via arrangement with The Robert Deis Archive. © 2017 Subtropic Productions, LLC. All rights reserved. The editors can be contacted at WeaselsRippedMyBook@gmail.com

BY ROBERT DEIS

"I had a glimpse of a squirrel perched on his neck; it seemed funny as hell for a second . . ."

That was the initial reaction of the main character in the story "Flying Rodents Ripped My Flesh" (pg. 31) when he saw a small furry creature land on his buddy in the Australian Outback. It's the same initial reaction most people have when they see the "killer flying squirrels" cover painting done by artist Wilbur "Wil" Hulsey for the August 1957 issue of *Man's Life* the story appeared in.

If you read that story and similar "killer creature" yarns from vintage men's adventure magazines, like those reprinted in this collection, you are likely to find out they aren't quite what you expected. Most animal attack stories in MAMs—including those that may initially seem like they'd be "funny as hell"—are dark action/adventure tales that are grim and *bloody* as hell. In most cases, they are essentially horror stories.

There are parallels in the realm of movies. The way for films like *The Birds* (1963), *Willard* (1971), *Frogs* (1972), *Jaws* (1975), *Grizzly* (1976) and many others was paved by killer creature stories in men's adventure magazines.

There are hundreds of such stories, involving every possible type of critter, from true potential maneaters like sharks, lions, and bears, to squirm-inducing species like snakes, scorpions, and spiders, to all kinds of critters that are highly unlikely threats to humans like weasels, squirrels, and anteaters.

(**Deis** *cont'd on pg. 4*)

HELL
in Men's Adventure Mags

BY WYATT DOYLE

The men's pulp adventure magazines published from the 1950s through the early '70s were not highbrow reading. They were downmarket, sensationalized entertainment for blue-collar readers. Packed with explosive action yarns and opinionated cultural exposés, accompanied by equally wild illustration art and photographs, MAMs enjoyed a well-deserved reputation for salaciousness and hyperbole.

The competition for readers was stiff, and the gloves were off. MAMs went big—often outrageously big, with outlandish stories published as true sometimes bordering on the surreal.

MAMs weren't respectable, but they were mainstream. And as periodicals calculated to attract a large but specific segment of the population, today MAMs offer unique perspectives on both the mid-20th century culture the magazines emerged from, as well as the under-documented interests and attitudes of the that era's working class, who the magazines were intended for. MAMs are artifacts of an era when significant numbers of blue-collar Americans still read for pleasure.

What's more, MAM illustration art and fiction, like so much visceral, "lowbrow" entertainment, remain potent and arresting today. None of this work was expected to be remembered for any longer than the time it took to read the magazine. Yet decades on, MAMs abilities to surprise, thrill, and entertain are undiminished.

Though MAMs are considered an evolution of the adventure pulp magazines of prior decades, MAMs are actually an outgrowth and distillation of *many* different kinds of male-focused periodicals, pulps

(**Doyle** *cont'd on pg.* 7)

(**Deis**, *cont'd from pg. 2*)

Man's Conquest March 1958,
art by George Gross

Man's Adventure January 1958,
art by Clarence Doore

In fact, animal attack stories are far more common in men's adventure magazines than stories about sadistic Nazis tormenting scantily clad women. Those outré Nazi stories are only common in the low-budget "sweat mag" subgenre of MAMs. Killer creature stories appeared at one time or another in most of the 160 different men's adventure titles published from the late 1940s to the late 1970s.

Many of those stories feature artwork by top illustration artists of the era. For example, the painting used for the first story in this book and featured on the cover was done by George Gross, an extremely-talented artist who started out doing cover paintings for the pre-World War II pulp fiction magazines that were forerunners of the MAM genre. Gross later did hundreds of cover and interior illustrations for men's adventure magazines and paperbacks.

His cover painting for the story "I Watched Them Eat Me Alive" is an eye-popping classic. But it's a lot less bloody than the story, which is not quite as far-fetched as you might think. Coconut crabs grow up to three feet across. Their claws, which can crush coconuts, can also easily slice

(**Doyle**, *cont'd from pg. 2*)

"I Battled a Giant Otter" *Men* December 1953, art by Robert Doares

among them. (True crime, detective, celebrity scandal, pinup photo, and outdoor sports magazines were also influences.) The MAM formula was to take what was already established, familiar, and popular among male readers, then amp up the sex, violence, and adrenaline. Hunting and fishing magazines had enjoyed wide male readership for decades, and regularly featured tales of wilderness survival, memorable hunting adventures, and accounts of excitement on the water—all ripe subjects for amplification in MAMs. Never a genre of half-measures, MAMs went on to publish *hundreds* of animal attack tales, where even the gentlest creatures turned mankiller for the sake of a good story—leading to some truly bizarre magazine covers. Ridiculous, trashy, excessive, and unlike anything else on newsstands, then or now. But those outlandish covers (by some of the finest commercial artists of the day) and lunatic concepts (by some of the most inventive hard-boiled writers ever to punch a typewriter), proved irresistible in their time, and remain irresistible today.

"We Couldn't Tear Them Off" *Hunting Adventures* Spring 1956, art by Tom Ryan

And while some scenarios seem laughable, the stories, taken on their own terms, are a different experience. Their horror is rooted in primal impulses, rational and irrational fears, and phobias of animals both large and small. There's rarely much in the way of moralizing. The victims aren't usually bad guys; often they're simply in the wrong place at the wrong time. Even those who survive are left maimed and deeply scarred by their ordeal, both physically and emotionally. Most stories end with the profoundly shaken narrator cataloging his missing body parts and describing the nightmares he still suffers. These sobering aspects of otherwise outrageous killer creature fiction take on unexpected resonance, considering MAM readership skewed heavily to veterans (then a significant percentage of the population) intimately familiar with comparable physical and emotional trauma acquired in real-world combat in World War II, Korea, and Vietnam.

It's not difficult to recognize the core appeal of these stories as metaphor to postwar male readers. Guys who'd seen the world, yet

"I Crawled With the Dragons"
For Men Only
April 1955,
art by Rafael DeSoto

Peril May 1958,
artist uncredited

Champ November 1957,
artist uncredited

frequently felt overcome by the hassles, adjustments, responsibilities, confusion, and uncertainty of life in fast-changing times. Guys who felt picked and pecked to pieces, acutely aware of each bite. Guys who sometimes felt like they were being eaten alive.

STORIES with outrageous premises demand complicity from the reader, via a willing suspension of disbelief—a blind trust that however strange the route may be, ultimately *thrills will be delivered.* Like campfire tales, MAM killer creature fiction is a brand of storytelling where a reader's engagement is often in direct proportion to the writer's enthusiasm. A committed narrative encourages committed reading, and a reader's imagination expands accordingly. Aiding that suspension of disbelief, MAMs maintained a consistent solemnity in presentations of persecution and torture, even as those torments were relished and fetishized. But no matter how outrageous the scenario, the fantasy was never interrupted by a wink from the author; MAM writers played it straight.

In "Flying Rodents Ripped My Flesh," the anthropologist narrator introduces the squirrel attack with the admission that "in some grotesque way it actually seemed funny." *Funny as hell.* But the subsequent description of being swarmed by a mass of small, hungry rodents is dark, vivid stuff, and the bite-by-bite account pulls few punches:

"On my neck there landed one especially tenacious squirrel, and every time I grabbed for it, it bit into my throat, darting back and forth squealing. Blood surged down from my cheeks as squirrels perched on my shoulders, slashed diabolically at my eyes. I felt a brush of fur against my mouth and bit down and felt a rake of claws groove my tongue…"

Hell, for sure. Funny? Only from a safe distance.

In 1960, *Psycho* author Robert Bloch, whose stories sometimes appeared in MAMs, published an essay in *Rogue,* a bachelor mag with occasional MAM elements. (The piece was subsequently abridged and reprinted in two parts by Forrest J Ackerman in *Famous Monsters of Filmland.*) The essay, "The Clown at Midnight," touches on the author's definitions of horror, and its title comes from a memorable quote by Lon Chaney that Bloch considered "the essence of true horror":

"A clown is funny in the circus ring, but what would be the normal reaction to opening a door at midnight and finding the same clown standing there in the moonlight?"

Perhaps killer creature stories—sometimes preposterous, often outrageous, even silly at first blush—are the MAMs' clowns at midnight. The imaginative reader opens the door at their own risk. ●

All Man November 1959, art by Clarence Doore

the clack of KILLER

Man's Life July 1957, artist uncredited

Man's Life September 1956, art by Clarence Doore

CRUSTACEANS

"Trapped in a Sea of Giant Crabs" *Man's Life* January 1958, art by Wil Hulsey

"I Watched Them Eat Me Alive"

STORY BY STAN SMITH   ART BY GEORGE GROSS

I WATCHED THEM

THE SNAPPING OF BONE AND THE PAIN LANCING INTO MY ARMPITS JOLTED ME AWAKE — AND THE FINGERS CAME OFF MY HAND!

by *LUDER KOOMANS*

as told to Stan Smith

■ PROPERLY, I suppose, my story begins on the moonless night of July 8, 1942, when a surfaced Jap I-boat rammed a brace of torpedoes into *Lemadjang Tambora*, a 6,000 ton Dutchman streaking westward into Lingga Archipelago for Cape Datuk, Borneo.

Lemadjang Tambora died instantly, a pall of flame enveloping her as she cracked amidships and settled into a cold South China Sea—all but 11 of her 74-man crew dying with her. I was ship's quartermaster standing port wing-tip, twelve-to-six, but the explosions that racked the merchantman merely catapulted my body clear of the undertow so that I floated away.

Of her other survivors, three—I later heard—died during the night of varying causes: shark; internal hemorrhages; broken neck. But seven men were picked up the following afternoon by a British destroyer, and when they could speak, confessed a unanimous belief that they were the sole personnel who had not perished. In a sense they were right—I was yet to be eaten by the giant crabs of the Badas Islands, a far more horrifying end than drowning, I assure you.

Throughout the night I clung desperately to a splint of boom that surged at dawn into the sharp tidal sweep of a small atoll and pitched me bodily onto white coral sands beneath a fringe of twisted palms. And there, exhausted completely, I slept for many hours.

I awoke at dusk, my shirt and pants dried   (*Please turn to page 56*)

Properly, I suppose, my story begins on the moonless night of
July 8, 1942, when a surfaced Jap I-boat rammed a brace of torpedoes
into *Lemadjang Tambora,* a 6,000 ton Dutchman streaking westward into
Lingga Archipelago for Cape Datuk, Borneo.

Lemadjang Tambora died instantly, a pall of flame enveloping her
as she cracked amidships and settled into a cold South China Sea—all
but 11 of her 74-man crew dying with her. I was ship's quartermaster
standing port wingtip, twelve-to-six, but the explosions that racked the
merchantman merely catapulted my body clear of the undertow so that I
floated away.

Of her other survivors, three—I later heard—died during the night
of varying causes: shark; internal hemorrhages; broken neck. But seven
men were picked up the following afternoon by a British destroyer, and
when they could speak, confessed a unanimous belief that they were
the sole personnel who had not perished. In a sense they were right—I
was yet to be eaten by the giant crabs of the Badas Islands, a far more
horrifying end than drowning, I assure you.

Throughout the night I clung desperately to a splint of boom that
surged at dawn into the sharp tidal sweep of a small atoll and pitched
me bodily onto white coral sands beneath a fringe of twisted palms. And
there, exhausted completely, I slept for many hours.

I awoke at dusk, my shirt and pants dried to my body, my throat
parched and my body incredibly stiff and aching. I could see the dragon
leaves of the darker inner verdure beyond the trees, so I climbed the bank

and began walking, believing somewhere I'd find fresh water.

For a while I was filled with an overwhelming remorse for my shipmates. I wondered whether I was the only one alive; I wondered whether any of the boats had been launched; I wondered why I was alive. But the immediacy of my plight took hold and for the moment, anyway, I forgot *Lemadjang Tambora* and walked barefoot over the sharp coral sands toward the peripheral green. I found no spring, and in little more than one hour, covered the entire atoll and returned to my starting point.

Suddenly I stared down at my feet, cursing myself for a fantastic stupidity. Coconuts! Coconuts on top of coconuts! I crashed one atop another and the tepid milky ooze surged into my hands. For long minutes I indulged my thirst and made my ablutions and feasted. Then I walked along the east shore thinking about shelter and a vantage point to search for ships. Again, the palms of the atoll served to console me. I promptly made a bed of crushed frond in the lee of the wind. In the morning, I planned to tie my shirt midpoint of a large tree trunk and wait. Sooner or later, I was convinced I'd be seen—for in those days there were many ships, junks to cruisers, threading the Badas Group daily. I was really unconcerned for my safety that evening as I munched a coconut dinner and started out over the vast, silken Lingga Archipelago. I was convinced someone would find me, and at dark I pulled the fronds over my body and fell again into a deep sleep.

Once during the night I heard a prolonged scratching sound above me high in the tree. I opened my eyes and stared upward but saw nothing other than a skyful of stars and a mackerel sky. Nerves! I grunted aloud. Waterlogged nerves stirring up the imagination—go back to sleep, Koomans!

I couldn't, though. I had the weirdest feeling there was something in the tree above me. I climbed out of my fronds, stood up and walked around. I saw nothing irregular so I chided myself and stretched out again, hands cupped behind my head, and I thought of home. I was then 29, married, two children. With the capture of Java, my family had been interned by the Japanese. Only a handful of natives and Dutchmen remained to run the desperate gamut of gunboats into the open sea in defiance of the Nippon. But for two complete runs, we of *Lemadjang Tambora* had done this—first with refugees and military personnel, and finally with cargo earmarked for the British, hove to in the Tambelian Group.

When they find me, I thought, I'll rejoin the Dutch on another ship. Isn't there always another somewhere? In a way, the idea amused me, too, for down deep I hated the sea. I was a farmer turned quartermaster by a sense of patriotism, little else; I'd left 80 acres at Tjilatjap because of the Nip invasion and the only thing I really wanted was to return home.

I leaned up on one elbow, staring out at the white water breaking on the reef and watched it coruscating under the mottled sky; and for a long minute, I heard only the boom of the surf, and it soothed me. Then night became day, and there was another surf soon.

I climbed out of the fronds, cracked a coconut and had myself a long drink, after which I began to scrape off some of the caked oil from my skin. It was hot that morning on the open atoll, but I walked around the length of it looking for signs of life. I found only the scattered pieces of wreckage.

I suddenly thought of the many cartoons one sees of the shipwrecked sailor lying around with a blonde under each arm, a jug of whiskey and a parrot. No such luxuries befell me. All I had was coconut juice and by now I was quite willing to start forgetting coconuts, in any shape. But I was far from discouraged because I figured that somewhere out on that broad expanse of Archipelago a ship would come and find me.

I picked the tallest tree facing the open sea which, coincidentally, was the one I'd slept under, then took off my shirt and looked up. The tree was about 60 feet to the knob of fronds and coconuts. I could get halfway up without much difficulty and I figured that to be enough.

I remember how I felt then before I went up, before the man-eating crabs began dining on fingers. I remember I felt good sitting at the trunk, staring out over the blue surf and imagining I could see the spindly cross-braces of a ship beyond the pall of sunhaze. I supposed all men cast adrift on lumps of coral felt as I did, imagining form in shadow, believing an optical illusion to be real and palpable. Yet, as much as I realized I was wishful thinking then, I could scarcely tear my eyes away from what I thought I saw on the horizon.

For almost an hour I watched it becoming sharper and more clearly defined. Then, forcibly I closed my eyes and prayed aloud that it was not an illusion. I held the shirt in my hands and I thought, Koomans, it's funny—how you hated this blue sailor shirt at one time! Now, maybe it's saving your life. I guess I mumbled like an insane man for a while there,

"Crawling Death of Bad Luck Island" *Stag* October 1955, art by Bob Schulz

staring alternately at the shirt and then at the hallucination. Christ! If I'm all upset now, how will it be in a month from now? Perish the thought, I groaned, imagine a steady diet of coconuts for a bloody month!

I barked my knee on the trunk of the tree, swore vehemently and began to shinny. I went slowly because as curved as it was, it was also one helluva lot of tree and when I reached the midway point I thought it wasn't high enough, so I climbed more yet.

Two thirds of the way up I stopped and pulled the shirt from over my shoulder and began fastening it by the sleeves. It happened then. Something moved above me and I raised my eyes and stared incredulously as a huge crab—big as a man's shoe—slowly began descending along the tree toward me. I was still tying the knot, and now frantically, as a clacking sound wafted into my head. Then more clacking sound—then I screamed as something lanced through my elbow and began grinding into my arm, and I fell.

I went down and the breath was knocked out of me, but I didn't roll, nor did I lose consciousness then. I was sick with terror as I lifted my arm and saw great rivulets of blood spurt into the air. My arm was gashed to the wrist, deep, yet again I heard the sound; but I could only lay there, writhing, grunting like some demented animal and look upward.

I could see the shirt, and the crabs—the immense robber crabs of the China Sea that live on coconuts and men's flesh—and the tree was swarming with them! I tasted blood in my throat as I raised my head and tried frantically to stand.

I was up on one leg as the waves of nausea and blackness engulfed me, and I felt myself sprawling headlong into the white sand. Reality faded and with it the tapping sound of claws, and the weird scratching of hard shell bodies running down the tree trunk.

It was the searing agony of pincer claws ripping through my hands I knew first as consciousness returned. I screamed as I felt the snapping of bone and pain lancing into my armpits. My body felt afire and I bolted upright shrieking, waving my hands trying to shake them off. They crawled over my legs, pulling pieces of flesh, skewering me. Blood spanked out over the sand as I hurled myself up and began jumping and screaming, beating them and pushing them off my chest and arms, and then the fingers of my right hand came off.

I could see three of them fighting over my fingers, scratching, hooking the fingers and running with them like a football player with the ball. My fingers! I tried to hold the hands up and I moaned and almost fainted again, but managed to brush one crab from my chest and stumble toward the surf.

Endlessly I screamed as they crawled toward me—dozens of them heavy as 10-pound weights with shiny black bodies and claws round as saucers. I had only the stump of a thumb on my right hand and no fingers at all on my left, but I used what I had to club them. Even as I fell again, weak from loss of blood and the sheer monstrous terror of it all, I scrambled on my rump toward the water. But the crabs followed me, slowly and relentlessly until I thought I would never overcome those last few yards.

I looked at my hands and cried and shrieked as I saw the thick redness gushing from purple veins that flopped over limply like dead worms; I saw bone—grey bone where there had been a left ankle; I saw the skin of my chest laid down like the blubber of a whale's belly; I felt the water coming up under my body and stared mutely as it became red and warm with my life.

My head tilted backward and I slid under, praying for death but I didn't stay down. God only knows why I forced myself to the surface, to sit there and stare at the dark line of robber crabs fringing the shore. But sit and stare I did in warm, waist high water, moaning incoherently and trying to hold my fingerless hands together.

And in that manner I was found by four Sumatrans in a fishing dhow. They had come to pick up wreckage as was their custom those days. But I knew nothing of this, nor anything else for three months; I was out of my mind from shock. I felt no sensation of any type as they lifted my body from the water and swaddled me in burlap.

I was taken to the island of Singkep in the Berhala Straits where both hands were amputated beneath the wrists. In other parts of my body I received almost 400 stitches, and quarts and quarts of plasma. I have no idea why the Japanese doctors who saved my life bothered to do so. Perhaps it was the novelty of so completely a degraded human; I can't say, really. I can only say I wish I'd gone down with *Lemadjang Tambora*— that kind of death would have been a far more merciful one. ●

"Curved Beaks Tore My Flesh" *True Men* STORIES October 1957

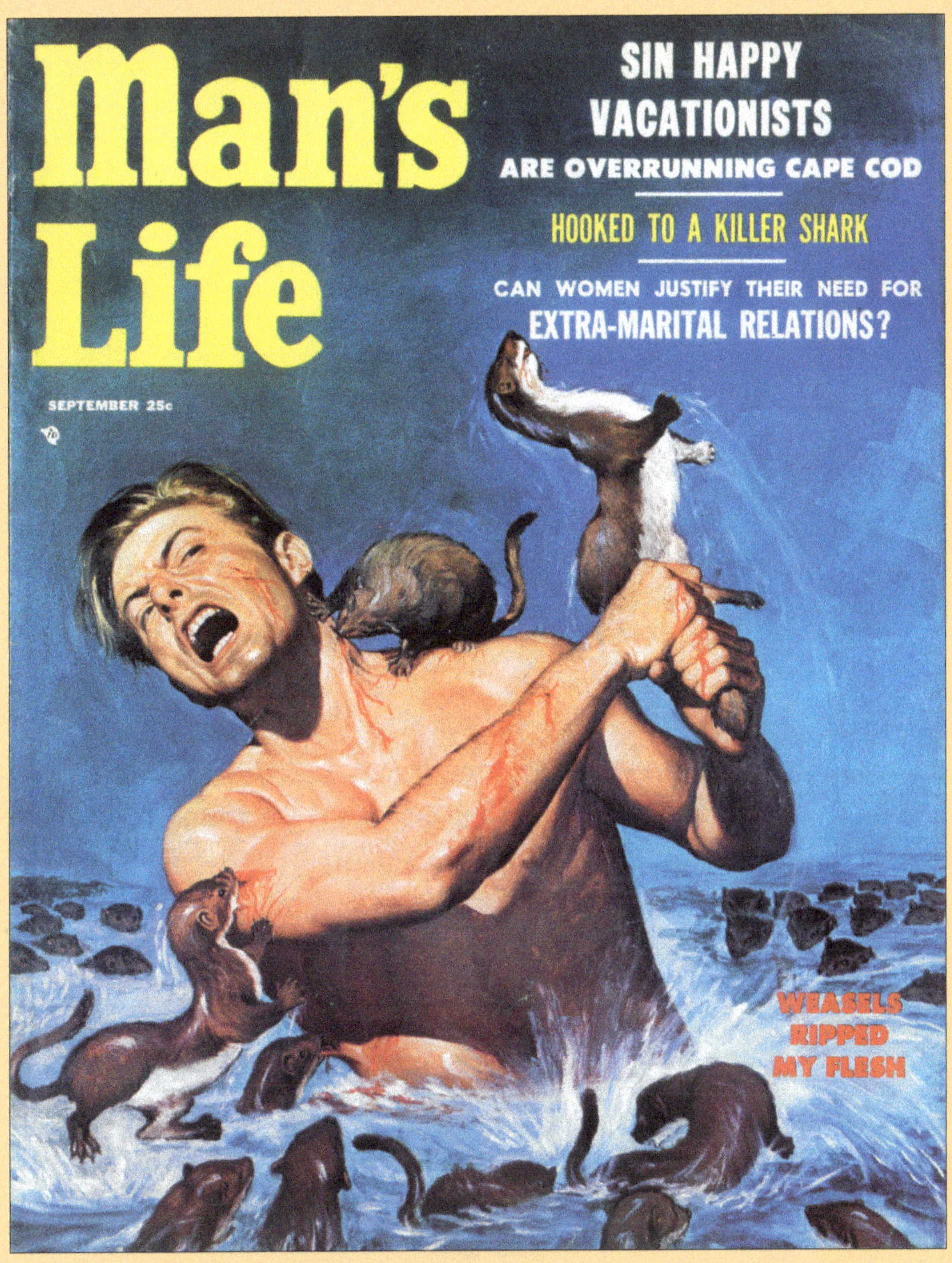

"Weasels Ripped My Flesh" *Man's Life* September 1956

Even *if the only animal attack cover artist Wil Hulsey ever painted had been the "Weasels Ripped My Flesh" art for the September 1956* Man's Life, *his place in the men's adventure pantheon would be assured. His style is smooth, tight, and realistic, even though the scenes he depicted are often fantastic. His colors are especially lush.*

Man's Life November 1955

Man's Life November 1957

Hulsey painted at least 20 great killer creature covers, and proved a master of the subject. He did work in several other categories as well, including exotic adventure pieces, Civil War scenes, and Westerns. His work appeared on issues of Man's Life and True Men Stories from the mid-1950s until about 1962.

Man's Life July 1958

Man's Life April 1959

"Chewed Alive and Screaming" *True Men* February 1959

In most Hulsey paintings, the focus is on foreground action, not sweeping panoramic vistas. Women in Hulsey's covers are often (barely) wearing a blazing red blouse or dress; that use of hot colors enhanced the eye-grab potential of the magazines' covers and, along with generous displays of cleavage, helped ensure an issue would pop on newsstands—in more ways than one.

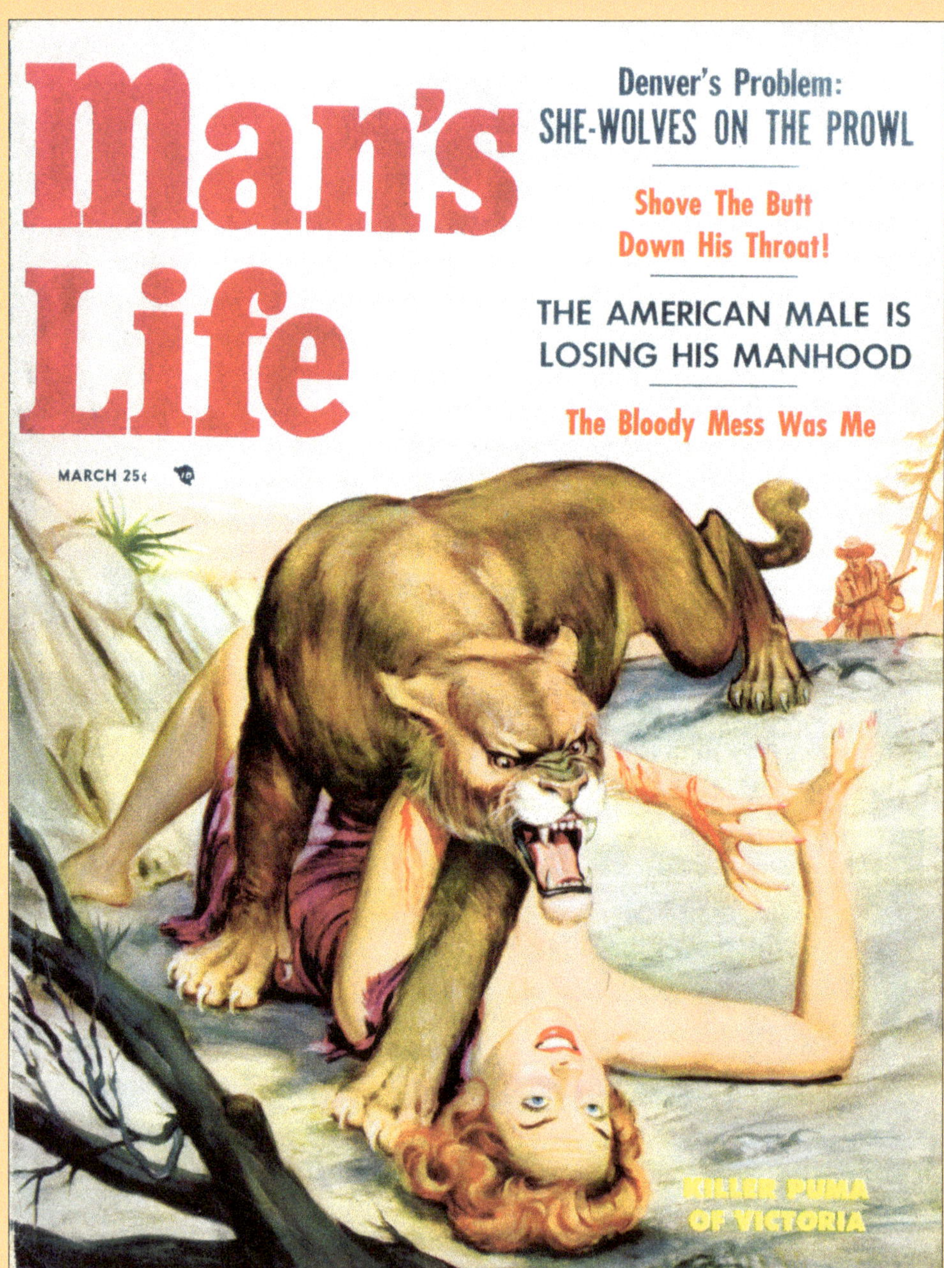

"Killer Puma of Victoria" *Man's Life* March 1957

"Killer With Short Tusks"
True Men Stories
June 1959

**"The Big Blonde and
the Black Beast Ripper"**
True Men Stories
September 1961

"Trapped in the Web of Creeping Death" *Man's Life* March 1959

"Flying Rodents Ripped My Flesh"

STORY BY LLOYD PARKER   ART BY WIL HULSEY

FLYING RODENTS RIPPED MY FLESH

by GEORGE RYERSON

as told to Lloyd Parker

Squealing and clawing, they tore flesh from bone, digging sharp teeth into him until his face was a red mask of terror —I tried to help him but monstrosities came down on me, and I began to die

Teeth like hot needles lanced my face and I shrieked as my skin came away in shreds.

BELLOWING, his hands clawing at the nape of his neck, Greco surged out of the deep clump of tif beyond the clearing, stumbling toward me. For a second I thought he'd lost his mind. I stood rooted, motionless, watching him.

"Run, George! In heaven's name, run!" Greco shrieked, sprawling on his belly. Inconceivable terror marred the handsome burnished face, yet in some grotesque way it actually seemed funny. I had a glimpse of a squirrel perched on his neck; it seemed funny as hell for a second.

The sun was a yellow brassy orb shining pleasantly on the river brush. There were no Arnhem cannibals on his tail, no nothing except squirrels! He was an easy fifty yards away when other brown, furred things began flying toward him. Small, they appeared and reappeared at his neck. Greco shrieked, "Run! Don't stand there, *run!*"

A weird fantasy of sight and sound filled the air around him. Locking at my partner's throat were flying squirrels, locking, biting his shielding hands. I ran toward him, ran as though his life depended on it. It was the second mistake we made.

"How'd you like scrambled eggs, old boy?" my partner grinned a few minutes before.

"Sure," I nodded. "I'd like a breast of duckling bigarde too. Where do you keep it?"

"There, Ryerson!" Greco beamed, pointing. "There's your first square meal in three months. See? Swamp goose!"

"You stay here. I don't want to frighten him. Too many feet in the bog, y'know—"

I'd never thought I'd see the day when a man would happily put his life on the line for a goose, or eggs. But that was one time, and it *was* certainly understandable, things considered.

WE'D just broken camp and were waiting near a salt water estuary for our native guides to bring in a log equipment float for the trip down the Lockhart River, in north Arnhem Land.

From cannibals to flying, furred death, the no man's land of Arnhem boasted 'em all. It was March 1950, and Greco and I, anthropologists, were the only white men within a thousand miles of that forgotten civilization.

Greco had been there before. He'd stocked us heavily with as many delicacies (eggs) as possible, but time, rain storms and a few other emergencies had us on basic rations. In a nutshell, anything that would go down and stay down.

OUR camp was at Camp York Peninsula, a good float trip up the Lockhart. Uncharted country for the most part, yet it was not entirely unknown. There had been several expeditions before, and the

Japs, much to their regret, had stationed a corps of tough China veterans in the area to watch for Allies.
In that immediate area they bivouacked, and it was there Arnhem
Landers quietly and thoroughly reduced their ranks. And ate them.

Usually the victims were felled by
spear or poisoned arrow. Meat was
then separated from bones, left to
dry, and stored in a wicket that the
cannibals wore around their necks.
We—Greco and I—managed a nice
social rapport with the islanders,
but every time I found myself in
company with one of them *at dinner*,
I had a hell of a time not vomiting.
One old man estimated he'd devoured 41 Japanese during the brief
stay of an occupation force. His best
meal was a plump Lieutenant General, and he had the medals and
insignia to prove it!

For a period of three months, my
associate and I had lived native, collecting data and specimens of everything from stone age fire implements
to obscure insects. We'd had a fair
share of croc scares, moana lizard
attacks (goanna) and more than
one informal visit by *Acanthophis
antarcticus*, the blunt-nosed death
adder whose venom is considered 50
times more potent than the Indian
cobra's. But for these horrors we
were prepared.

THE Ngillpidgi people with whom
we lived were eager enough to
help us. With the utmost impunity
we went about our business of collecting specimens, sharing with them
the fruits of our rifle kills, and so
on. The only thing we tried to do
apart from the Ngillpidgi was to *eat*.
I liked to *know* what sort of meat
was in the cookpot, and aside from
the couple of state dinners we had
to attend, diligently kept to my own
menu. It wasn't much, but at least
I was reasonably sure it wasn't
human.

Food was a pretty precarious business, but like anything else one adjusted after a while. Even conical
breasted, semi-nude islanders one
became accustomed to. They weren't
exactly bathing beauties but after
three months they weren't the ugliest women in the world, either. A
place of stone age civilization, incredibly severe weather, remorseless
jungle, Arnhem Land, Australia's
northern geographical wonder, offered much to my partner and me.
Just about the only thing it didn't
offer was a square meal, and at the
time, a goose egg omelet seemed like
a wonderful idea.

I HEARD John Greco thrashing in
the waist deep grass beyond the
clearing, heard his elated shout. He
not only had the eggs, he had what
laid 'em. But, a moment later, he
reappeared, hands clawing at the
back of his neck, bellowing like
crazy. I thought he'd lost his mind.

I stood there, motionless, staring at
him.

"Run, George! Run!" Greco wheezed, sprawling toward the clearing. I
thought it was some kind of ghastly
joke. When I first looked there was
nothing behind him, no crocodile,
no goanna, not even a head hunter.

Greco was a good fifty yards from
the clearing when the first flying
squirrel appeared perched on his
neck. Then another and another.
They seemed to cling there, as if
raking into his flesh, burrowing. His
face was a mask of incredible terror
as he sprawled toward me, flailing
away at the small, furred monstrosities perched there.

I got an option on eternity seconds
later as John Greco sagged into a
rut of blade edged tifi grass, screaming. Instead of running the other
way, I chose to help him—a noble,
prohibitively expensive gesture. A
cloud of squeaking flying devils took
to my body in a rush. The air was

filled with them and their noises.
Then, I too, began to die.

Ten yards from the fallen Greco,
rapier fangs slammed into my neck,
head and hands as I charged
through the grass. It was as if parachutes had been attached to the underpinnings of common squirrels.
Literally, they soared into the cloudless sky, claws distended, gyrating
forward, squeaking, button-eyes
blazing. I brought my hands over
my head and turned, as then, blood
streaming from his face, John Greco
closed behind me.

"The river! The river!" I howled,
plunging toward the clearing. Behind me, I heard only the unearthly
moaning of a man being eaten alive.
That is a sound. I know because I
heard it from my own lips.

SUDDENLY the ground shifted beneath my feet as a brown swarm
leaping straight up, attached itself
(*Continued on page 74*)

Bellowing, his hands clawing at the nape of his neck, Greco surged out of the deep clump of tifi beyond the clearing, stumbling toward me. For a second I thought he'd lost his mind. I stood rooted, motionless, watching him.

"Run, George! In heaven's name, run!" Greco shrieked, sprawling on his belly. Inconceivable terror marred the handsome burnished face, yet in some grotesque way it actually seemed funny. I had a glimpse of a squirrel perched on his neck; it seemed funny as hell for a second.

The sun was a yellow brassy orb shining pleasantly on the river brush. There were no Arnhem cannibals on his tail, no nothing except squirrels! He was an easy fifty yards away when other brown, furred things began flying toward him. Small, they appeared and reappeared at his neck. Greco shrieked, "Run! Don't stand there, *run!*"

A weird fantasy of sight and sound filled the air around him. Locking at my partner's throat were flying squirrels, locking, biting his shielding hands. I ran toward him, ran as though his life depended on it. It was the second mistake we made.

"How'd you like scrambled eggs, old boy?" my partner grinned a few minutes before.

"Sure," I nodded. "I'd like a breast of duckling bigarde too. Where do you keep it?"

"There, Ryerson!" Greco beamed, pointing. "There's your first square meal in three months. See? Swamp goose!"

"You stay here. I don't want to frighten him. Too many feet in the bog, y'know—"

I'd never thought I'd see the day when a man would happily put his life on the line for a goose, or eggs. But that was one time, and it was certainly understandable, things considered.

WE'D just broken camp and were waiting near a salt water estuary for our native guides to bring in a log equipment float for the trip down the Lockhart River, in north Arnhem Land.

From cannibals to flying, furred death, the no-man's land of Arnhem boasted 'em all. It was March 1950, and Greco and I, anthropologists, were the only white men within a thousand miles of that forgotten civilization.

Greco had been there before. He'd stocked us heavily with as many delicacies (eggs) as possible, but time, rain storms and a few other emergencies had us on basic rations. In a nutshell, anything that would go down and stay down.

OUR camp was at Camp York Peninsula, a good float trip up the Lockhart. Uncharted country, for the most part, yet it was not entirely unknown. There had been several expeditions before, and the Japs, much to their regret, had stationed a corps of tough China veterans in the area to watch for Allies. In that immediate area they bivouacked, and it was there Arnhem Landers quietly and thoroughly reduced their ranks. And ate them.

Usually the victims were felled by spear or poisoned arrow. Meat was then separated from bones, left to dry, and stored in a wicket that the cannibals wore around their necks. We—Greco and I—managed a nice social rapport with the islanders, but every time I found myself in company with one of them *at dinner*, I had a hell of a time not vomiting. One old man estimated he'd devoured 41 Japanese during the brief stay of an occupation force. His best meal was a plump Lieutenant General, and he had the medals and insignia to prove it!

For a period of three months, my associate and I had lived native, collecting data and specimens of everything from stone age fire implements to obscure insects. We'd had a fair share of croc scares, moana lizard attacks (goanna) and more than one informal visit by *Acanthophis antarctieus*, the blunt-nosed death adder whose venom is considered 50 times more potent than the Indian cobra's. But for these horrors we were prepared.

THE Ngillpidgi people with whom we lived were eager enough to help us. With the utmost impunity we went about our business of collecting specimens, sharing with them the fruits of our rifle kills, and so on. The only thing we tried to do apart from the Ngillpidgi was to eat. I liked to *know* what sort of meat was in the cookpot, and aside from the couple of state dinners we had to attend, diligently kept to my own menu. It wasn't much, but at least I was reasonably sure it wasn't human.

Food was a pretty precarious business, but like anything else one adjusted after a while. Even conical breasted, semi-nude islanders one became accustomed to. They weren't exactly bathing beauties, but after three months they weren't the ugliest women in the world, either. A place of stone age civilization, incredibly severe weather, remorseless jungle, Arnhem Land, Australia's northern geographical wonder, offered much to my partner and me. Just about the only thing it didn't offer was a square meal, and at the time, a goose egg omelet seemed like a wonderful idea.

I HEARD John Greco thrashing in the waist deep grass beyond the clearing, heard his elated shout. He not only had the eggs, he had what laid 'em. But, a moment later, he reappeared, hands clawing at the back of his neck, bellowing like crazy. I thought he'd lost his mind.

I stood there, motionless, staring at him.

"Run, George! Run!" Greco wheezed, sprawling toward the clearing. I thought it was some kind of ghastly joke. When I first looked there was nothing behind him, no crocodile, no goanna, not even a headhunter.

Greco was a good fifty yards from the clearing when the first flying squirrel appeared perched on his neck. Then another and another. They seemed to cling there, as if raking into his flesh, burrowing. His face was a mask of incredible terror as he sprawled toward me, flailing away at the small, furred monstrosities perched there.

I got an option on eternity seconds later as John Greco sagged into a rut of blade edged tifi grass, screaming. Instead of running the other way, I chose to help him—a noble, prohibitively expensive gesture. A cloud of squeaking flying devils took to my body in a rush. The air was filled with them and their noises. Then, I too, began to die.

"The Island of Man-Eating Rats" *Man's Life* May 1956, art by Wil Hulsey

Ten yards from the fallen Greco, rapier fangs slammed into my neck, head and hands as I charged through the grass. It was as if parachutes had been attached to the underpinnings of common squirrels. Literally, they soared into the cloudless sky, claws distended, gyrating forward, squeaking, button-eyes blazing. I brought my hands over my head and turned, as then, blood streaming from his face, John Greco closest behind me.

"The river! The river!" I howled, plunging toward the clearing. Behind me, I heard only the unearthly moaning of a man being eaten alive. *That* is a sound. I know because I heard it from my own lips.

SUDDENLY, the ground shifted beneath my feet as a brown swarm leaping straight up, attached itself to my chest. Running, I was aware only of my own yelling. Soft, warm bodies squirmed in my grasp, clinging to my skin as I frantically tore at them. Strips of flesh pulled away as incisors begged in like hot drills, grinding and squealing until the sound of them was louder than my voice.

On my neck there landed one especially tenacious squirrel, and every time I grabbed for it, it bit into my throat, darting back and forth squealing. Blood surged down from my cheeks as squirrels perched on my shoulders, slashed diabolically at my eyes. I felt a brush of fur against my mouth and bit down and felt a rake of claws groove my tongue.

Inside my trousers, on both legs, those squirrels weighted me like sinkers, tore through the fabric and burrowed through pants and legs. I was alive with needle pains, hot and endless as my flesh came away in shreds. I fell, not tripping, but weighted down. I fell on my stomach, aware of squirming as I rolled over, frantically trying to disgorge them from my throat. Whenever fur flashed against my mouth I bit, eyes closed, feeling the savage reprisals lancing my face. I caught one in the middle, holding it lengthwise, screaming insanely as it thrashed in my grasp. I watched, delighted, as I squeezed a mass of blood and gray gore through its mouth, and felt it bursting in my hand.

ON MY feet, I stumbled blindly toward the river, hacking at myself, pulling them like leeches—and where one would disappear I would pull another. I couldn't see for the spate of crimson flooding down my scalp blurred in my eyes. I touched the top of my head and felt a numbness in my right hand. The fingers of one hand were bitten off at the end joints; the fingers of the other were gnawed to the bone. In my shoes, the wet moisture of falling blood reminded me of my childhood when I'd fallen in a pond fully dressed. I was drenched with my own blood, stumbling frenziedly to a raft that I knew was there yet couldn't see.

Greco was lucky. He died quickly. When he went down for the last time, the flying shredded death covered him like a blanket and bit through his windpipe. I died a slower death, much slower.

The river splashed beneath my boots and I fell in, headlong, ducking, throwing off some of the furred death; drowning the more obdurate that either deliberately clawed up my head or couldn't get out of my trousers. I thrashed to the surface and somehow managed to lie in the shallows, momentarily immune.

MY BODY—what there was left of it—spewed my blood into the murky Lockhart. I remembered the crocodiles, and the panic of that brought a semblance of consciousness. I wiped the blood from my eyes and swam to the raft, there to wait, praying for enough strength to pull myself aboard.

Until dusk I lay on the raft. I was found, a mouthful of fur, a body full of holes, dying outstretched on palms. For four weeks a search party combed the Roper District of Arnhem, thirty miles away, unable to locate me. My aboriginal friend, a guide, secreted me into the mountain colony where other natives dressed my wounds in panadus leaves and with the medications of their own device. I was found only when my guide brought me down-river in a burial canoe, the end was that near.

I lost both hands to the wrists, a slice of my left buttock, and most of my scalp. And the vision of my right eye. That, too. There were a thousand deaths on Arnhem Land but ours was the worst. Not even a cannibal stew pot could quite compare with it. It was—as Arnhem Land is even today—something out of the next world; something out of a world time forgot, but an anthropologist's paradise. John Greco, I'm sure, would agree. ●

GORILLAS

Safari August 1957,
artist uncredited

True Men Stories October 1956,
art by Wil Hulsey

at large

Safari February 1956, art by M.L. Bower

Man's Adventure March 1961, art by Norm Eastman

Animal Life May 1954, art by Clarence Doore

"I Hunted the Gorilla of Yamaken" *Hunting Adventures* Fall 1955, art by Jim Bentley

"Terror Safari"

STORY BY LESTER HUTTON   ART BY JOHN DUILLO

TERROR
SAFARI

By LESTER HUTTON

IT WAS ALL too close for comfort. The giant gorilla was still 30 feet above us in the tree, but the tree was not more than 50 feet away from Mogano and me. The Landrovers were only about 100 feet to our left. Still we couldn't shoot till he put down the native girl. She was slung across his shoulder, and she was still alive because we could hear her moan, but she no longer struggled, and blood from an ugly gash on her head was streaked down her shoulders and across her half-naked brown body.

Then suddenly with a roar of rage he dropped through the branches, let the girl's inert form slip to the ground and lumbered through the bushes at us. He was coming fast and fiercely, and as he emerged from the underbrush I saw he was over nine feet high and looked as wide as a car. The giant swinging arms and huge shoulders and open-mouthed, bellowing, angry head rushed toward me like a charging bull.

The rifle had been on him since he left the tree, however, and as soon he appeared through the underbrush I squeezed the trigger. The roar of the gun and a roar of rage from him echoed together with another explosion. There was a flash of white light from the left, and he swerved and I realized too late what had gone wrong.

Martha had used a flash bulb in her camera and it made him jump and my shot and Mogano's missed, and then he saw the beautiful girl in the Landrover and went bowling through the brush at the car. It was unbelievable and terrifying. He hit the Landrover in a rush with eyes only for the girl, and she and the scattered natives were tumbled like toys as he actually upended the vehicle, and it rocked over on its side.

I couldn't shoot but I was screaming and running right after his broad back, and I saw him literally pluck her out of the

(continued on page 43)

9

It was all too close for comfort. The giant gorilla was still 30 feet above us
in the tree, but the tree was not more than 50 feet away from Mogano and
me. The Landrovers were only about 100 feet to our left. Still, we couldn't
shoot till he put down the native girl. She was slung across his shoulder,
and she was still alive because we could hear her moan, but she no longer
struggled, and blood from an ugly gash on her head was streaked down
her shoulders and across her half-naked brown body.

Then suddenly with a roar of rage he dropped through the branches,
let the girl's inert form slip to the ground and lumbered through the
bushes at us. He was coming fast and fiercely, and as he emerged from
the underbrush I saw he was over nine feet high and looked as wide as
a car. The giant swinging arms and huge shoulders and open-mouthed,
bellowing, angry head rushed toward me like a charging bull.

The rifle had been on him since he left the tree, however, and as soon
he appeared through the underbrush I squeezed the trigger. The roar
of the gun and a roar of rage from him echoed together with another
explosion. There was a flash of white light from the left, and he swerved
and I realized too late what had gone wrong.

Martha had used a flash bulb in her camera and it made him jump
and my shot and Mogano's missed, and then he saw the beautiful girl
in the Landrover and went bowling through the brush at the car. It was
unbelievable and terrifying. He hit the Landrover in a rush, with eyes
only for the girl, and she and the scattered natives were tumbled like toys
as he actually upended the vehicle, and it rocked over on its side.

I couldn't shoot but I was screaming and running right after his broad back, and I saw him literally pluck her out of the air from the rocking Landrover as it was going over. Then he was clear of it with Martha in his huge arms and she was screaming and clawing at him in a kind of ultimate hysteria, her beautiful face contorted with terror.

I swung the rifle butt at his head as he wheeled on me. He caught it in one hand and twisted it away from me. Then a back-sweep of the same huge hand exploded stars in my head, and I felt my feet leave the ground as I went several feet through the air. I ran reeling after him, thinking my skull was crushed and seeing stars and spinning trees and guided mainly by her helpless voice still screaming.

I don't know what kept me on my feet but the image of her terrified face and that huge obscene head of his next to it. I leaped on his back from behind and swung the hunting knife in my hand in a wide arc at his shoulders. There was a new roar of rage from him, and I felt hot blood on my hand, and then he caught me by the left arm and fire exploded in my shoulder as I sailed some eight feet through the air, and as consciousness faded I thought, "He's got her and my arm's torn off . . ." Then I hit the tree trunk and went black, entirely thinking but not quite certain that he had swung into a tree carrying Martha and disappeared.

I EXPECTED trouble when I agreed to take the all-female group on safari, but not the kind of trouble I found. There were six rich American women, four of them married, but all out for kicks, and a seventh who was neither out for kicks nor rich, but was the kickiest one of the bunch as far as I was concerned. Her name was Martha Wilks, and she was a freelance photographer commissioned by one of the big magazines to come along and photograph the hijinks when a group of society women hire two white hunters to take them on an all-girl safari into the wilds of Kenya.

But I'm getting ahead of myself, just because I happened to have a personal interest in Martha. To begin at the beginning, my brother John and I were in Nairobi a few years back, before the Mau-Mau thing broke out and turned all of Kenya into blood and fire, and we were working as professional hunters and guides to hunting expeditions. We had grown up in the area, since our parents were missionaries there until World War II. And after our part in the service, John and I had decided to try a venture as pros, doing what we had done for years as amateurs.

We didn't make out too badly, and it was getting to be fun when we
got this wired contract. It came through a New York travel agency, and
the people picked us because, unlike most white hunters on the big game
circuit, we were not just individuals, but a firm with two members.

Two hunters were needed for this safari because it consisted of six
women and no men, and only two of the women had ever hunted before.
But they all wanted to go on safari, shoot big game like lions and water
buffalo, and get the whole treatment. Since they were novices and four
were complete strangers to hunting, they needed a complete caretaking
service, not just the usual kind of safari.

It was clearly a pain-in-the-neck operation, but they were paying
accordingly. It gave John and me a chance to go out together for several
weeks, and also to collect extraordinary fees. So—we grabbed it.

The addition of Martha Wilks, the photographer, was made later,
just before the safari got under way. The magazine had not decided on
assigning it to her until the last minute. Anyway, in May of 1950 we
started out, went northwest from Nairobi, heading toward the Kisumu on
the shores of Lake Victoria. The seven women were not as tough to take
care of as we had expected.

They did as told where safety precautions were concerned, got along
better together than we had anticipated, and made only the usual number
of passes, which (notwithstanding all you read about white hunters
brushing them off) were not particularly unwelcome. All seven of them
were at last attractive, and three of them were damned good-looking.
They were gay and casual about it, and when one of them began making
out very openly with my kid brother, nobody was jealous or catty. But
a couple of others continued to flirt with him, while the others took
their turns making passes at me. The only one who made none was the
photographer.

I wished she would. She was a tall, lithe brown-haired beauty with a
sense of humor and an easy, understanding smile that got under my skin.
She was also frankly feminine and did not hide the fact that, in her words,
she could "dig" me, but felt this was not her party. She stuck to taking
pictures and left the game, both wild and domesticated, to the ladies
who were paying for it. We did have a date for the first night the safari
was ended and we were back in Nairobi, but agreeing to that was as far
as she'd go while in the jungle. I spent a lot of time thinking about that

"Mating Raid of the Congo Killer" *Impact* August 1957, art by George Gross

night that was to come.

By and large things went well the first week. We got several antelope—a couple of which the girls really shot themselves—and two water buffs, one with considerable help from John and the other brought down largely by my shots. The ladies got shots into all of them, though, and laughingly claimed the trophies.

Then it happened, all in a matter of a few hours on the ninth day of the safari, but it seemed—and still does—like an eternity of nightmare, and now, 10 years later, it's still like a nightmare when I think about it, and of course I'm reminded every time I start to use my left arm.

We were traveling in three Landrovers, I was in the first with Mogano, our head man, driving, and two of the women in the back seat. Three of the girls were in the second one with a reliable gunbearer doing the driving, and John was driving the third with the other two women and two of our boys.

We came to a little village called Mbutu in mid-morning, and as we approached it, I saw immediately that something was wrong. There was nobody out in the small area of cleared fields, and not enough activity in the village. As we pulled closer, I saw the crowd at one end, clustered together and excited. When they saw us there were joyous shouts, and they rushed to us like we were bringing water during a drought.

The story was quickly and excitedly told. There was a bull gorilla on a rampage. He had stolen a 13-year-old girl from one of the fields just minutes before. But this was not, according to the terrified natives, like other gorillas gone wild. This one had gotten two women in the last 10 days and had passed up some small children and men to get to both of his victims. He was out for women—*only women.* It was crazy, but they stuck to the story. That didn't make sense. Gorillas don't fall for human dames, despite what they said in *King Kong*, and this ape wasn't out there in the bush raping that girl now.

But even the chief's young son, who was the pride of the village, a straight, tall youth of 22 with an intelligent manner and a first rate command of English, insisted the story was true.

He looked at me soberly and said in a low voice, "What they say is true. It is something different, this gorilla. Not like any I have seen. And big, very big."

I agreed to go for it, and leaving John to ride herd on the women there in the village where they would be safe, I took Mogano and one of the bearers and a group of the local men in two of the Landrovers and started in the direction the ape had taken when last seen. We had already gone a mile or more when I happened to look back and see Martha in the second Landrover, camera in hand, and an eager look on her beautiful puss. I yelled for Mogano to stop and went steaming back to the other car.

"What are you doing here," I yelled before I even got to the car. "I said I wanted all the women to stay back there."

She climbed out and I couldn't help noticing, even then, the movement of her long legs in the tight chino pants. She was grinning sheepishly, but there was a determined look around her wide beautiful mouth.

"Look, Ranse, these will be the best pictures of the whole business. And I'll stay out of your way. Honest." I just glared and she went on quickly, "Do I ever ask you to sleep with me 'cause the jungle sounds restless, or to wash my back when I bathe in the river like the other gals do? No. This is the first favor I've asked. Let me shoot you shooting the ape."

"I'd rather do you one of the other favors," I growled.

"You know, that could be arranged, too," she grinned again. "But seriously, let me shoot this—please."

"It's too late to go back now," I admitted. "But stay in the car. This is a big bull and he's nuts according to the boys."

She leaned forward and kissed me quickly. "Thanks, Doll." And she squeezed my arm, and added, "You be careful too, huh? You won't do me any good with a broken back."

I was still thinking about that kiss 15 minutes later when one of the men cried out and pointed and we had our first view of the monster. He was in a big tree a couple of hundred feet away and was holding the girl and gazing at her in a funny way for an ape, and suddenly I felt a cold prickle run down my back. It was silly, but for the first time I started thinking about what they had said, and wished Martha wasn't along. About that time he saw us coming and swung out on a limb carrying her like a newspaper under his arm, and I got a look at how big he really was.

It scared me. I'd faced lions and rhinos and gorillas before, but nothing like him. The slim form of the young girl seemed to move slightly, and that galvanized me into action. Maybe there was a chance, somehow, to get her away from him alive. I jumped out of the Landrover, and Mogano followed me, and several of the men followed him. The second Landrover followed close behind the group of us on foot.

The girl's body in his arms made shooting impossible, but the men spread out, making noise, hoping to excite him so he'd leave her, and Mogano and I hurried after him, waiting. Then came the moment we had been waiting for, when he put her down, came crashing through the underbrush and my world exploded with the burst of that flash bulb of Martha's.

I CAME to, conscious only of pain, searing pain in my left arm and shoulder. Then I remembered it all, and Martha, and I guess I almost went out of my head. I insisted on giving chase with the arm dangling, and the blood welling out of my gashed face and the pain in my shoulder like nothing I can put into words.

The hairy giant had not gotten far away because some of the spread out natives had surrounded him, and their numbers and noise had driven him into a little thicket. But all the problems were the same, only doubled in spades. We couldn't get a clear shot from far away because he now had Martha, and he was hidden from view and underbrush was too thick to do anything from outside it. We had to go in. Mogano tried to slow me down, but I ran ahead of him wildly, carrying the rifle in my one good arm, and I headed right into the thicket.

I was cursing and screaming and sobbing and groaning all at the same time, but I couldn't control it. I could hear Mogano shouting to the others to advance and help as he followed close behind me, but it was all very removed from me. The only things that were really getting through to me were that my shoulder was on fire and *the monster had Martha.*

She was lying still across a fallen tree and he was peering down at her when I saw him. As he wheeled around at the sound of my approach I saw that there was blood down the front of her and her blouse was all ripped, leaving one white shoulder and breast naked, and I went even madder. Lifting the point of the gun level with my one good hand, I rushed right up to him.

The small red-streaked eyes were gleaming furiously, and the big ugly mouth was open wide, drooling foam from the corners of the slack

"The Lady and the Gorilla" *Rage For Men* April 1957, art by Clarence Doore

lips as he let out a terrible bellow of rage. The great chest, matted with coarse dark hair, gleamed wetly, and I never knew whether it was with his sweat or his victims' blood. The muscles bulged in it and across the giant shoulders in hands as big as my thigh. He swung the great arms high and straightened up and charged, and towering over me, he brought down one club-like hand across my neck as I struggled to raise the muzzle of the rifle against the broad chest.

The crushing hand across my neck bludgeoned me backwards and the darkness closed in, and I knew I couldn't shake it off this time. I knew too that I hadn't gotten the muzzle up level with the one tired arm but I tried to squeeze the trigger anyway, but the big vice-like hand closed on my throat and jerked me backwards and the huge, roaring, hairy face rushed in with the darkness.

Again pain was the first consciousness that started up through the spinning, deep darkness. I was all agonized, crushed pulp, it felt like, and there seemed to be a great pulverizing pressure mashing the last life out of me. Then there was noise and excited voices and then Mogano's voice silencing, ordering, and then his face through my blurred vision looking down at me as something was being pulled at across my chest.

Then I was aware of the big, rough, heavy body on me just as it was lifted away, and somebody pulled the vice-like fingers from my neck, and Mogano put something wet on my face and called my name gently. I couldn't move, and everything in me, it felt like, was crushed and broken, but I was alive. Warm, wet blood was running down on me from the gorilla's body as a half dozen men lifting together tugged it off of me.

I was not sure I'd live until I heard Martha's sobbing voice repeating my name questioningly, and then saw her pull away from those trying to minister to her and run to my side. There was blood smeared on her face and her breasts were bared through the shreds of what had been her blouse, but she didn't care about any of that, nor about the mess I was.

In all the tortured, almost numb nerves of my body I felt her gentle hands going over me, saw her face with tears coursing down through the streaked blood close to mine peering into my eyes as she whispered my name. She was as beautiful as anything I've ever seen. And through all the blinding pain I felt some kind of comfort as she gathered my head gently into her hands and pressed my head against her cheek and held me softly against the smooth warm bosom.

I passed out again when they moved me back to the village, but it was with a dreamy awareness that I was still alive and had to live because she was. It was four days before I came to again, and weeks before they could move me. I still can't raise my left arm over my head, but otherwise I've got most of the use of it, and I'm happy to report I have the use of both of Martha's. She hasn't been away from me since then.

I got the big monkey through the lower belly and the groin as he hit me. I didn't get the muzzle of the rifle up level, but it was against him and I did pull the trigger as he clobbered me the last time.

My shot was enough to kill him, but he'd have squeezed my head off first if Mogano hadn't been right behind me and shot him again as he went over on top of me. That killed him instantly.

My left arm was torn almost completely out of the socket at the shoulder, but luckily there were enough muscles and tendons left to keep it on and make it work again after the doctor put it back together. Other than that I had only three fractured ribs, a cracked skull and four vertebrae in my neck and back fractured.

Martha got off easy. Only a slight concussion and two cracked ribs. They picked up the 13-year-old girl the ape had dropped and she had a broken back, but the doctor saved her. She walks a little stiffly now, but otherwise she's okay. They never found the first two victims the gorilla got.

My brother John managed to finish the safari with the ladies and Martha managed to photograph it after they got me back to the Nairobi hospital, so nobody lost any pay on the deal. And I got Martha out of the deal, so nobody went home empty-handed. She's all mine now, and I don't want to lose her, but I hope I never have to fight for her again with a killer gorilla. ●

A subset *of MAM killer creature stories feature artwork in which sadistic villains—Nazis, "Commies" (Chinese, Korean or Vietnamese Communists), Arabs, tribal natives of various lands—use animals to torment scantily clad damsels or hapless male captives. In vintage periodicals, torture-by-critter as a subgenre is virtually unique to MAMs.*

There is historical basis for some of those stories. But for publishers, selling magazines was the prime directive, not historical accuracy. To grab eyeballs at newsstands, MAMs went where no mags had gone before, with bizarre scenes of victims tormented with animals such as minks, monkeys, squids and iguanas. Many of the featured creatures are not really maneaters. Sometimes, they're not even meat eaters. Indeed, it would be nearly or totally impossible to get most of them to do the things shown in many MAM illustrations. But imagination-stretching scenarios are a hallmark of men's adventure mags.

Man's Action January 1963, art by Walter Popp

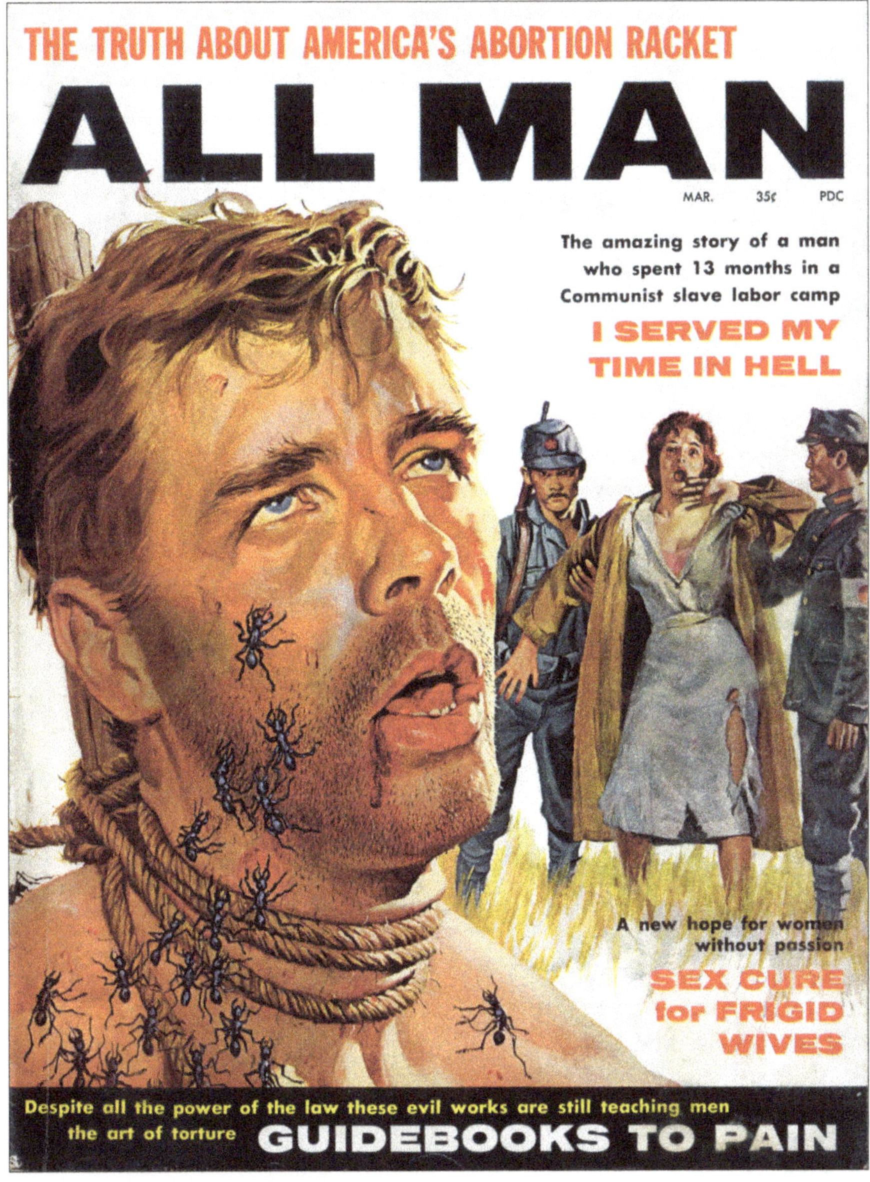

"I Served My Time in Hell" *All Man* March 1956, artist uncredited
(Artwork later reused to illustrate a story in Man's Best *September 1961)*

"1,000 Brides for Hitler's
Beast of Horror"
New Man
April 1964
art by Norman Saunders

"The Terrible Oriental
Mink Torturers!"
Wildcat Adventures
February 1961
artist uncredited

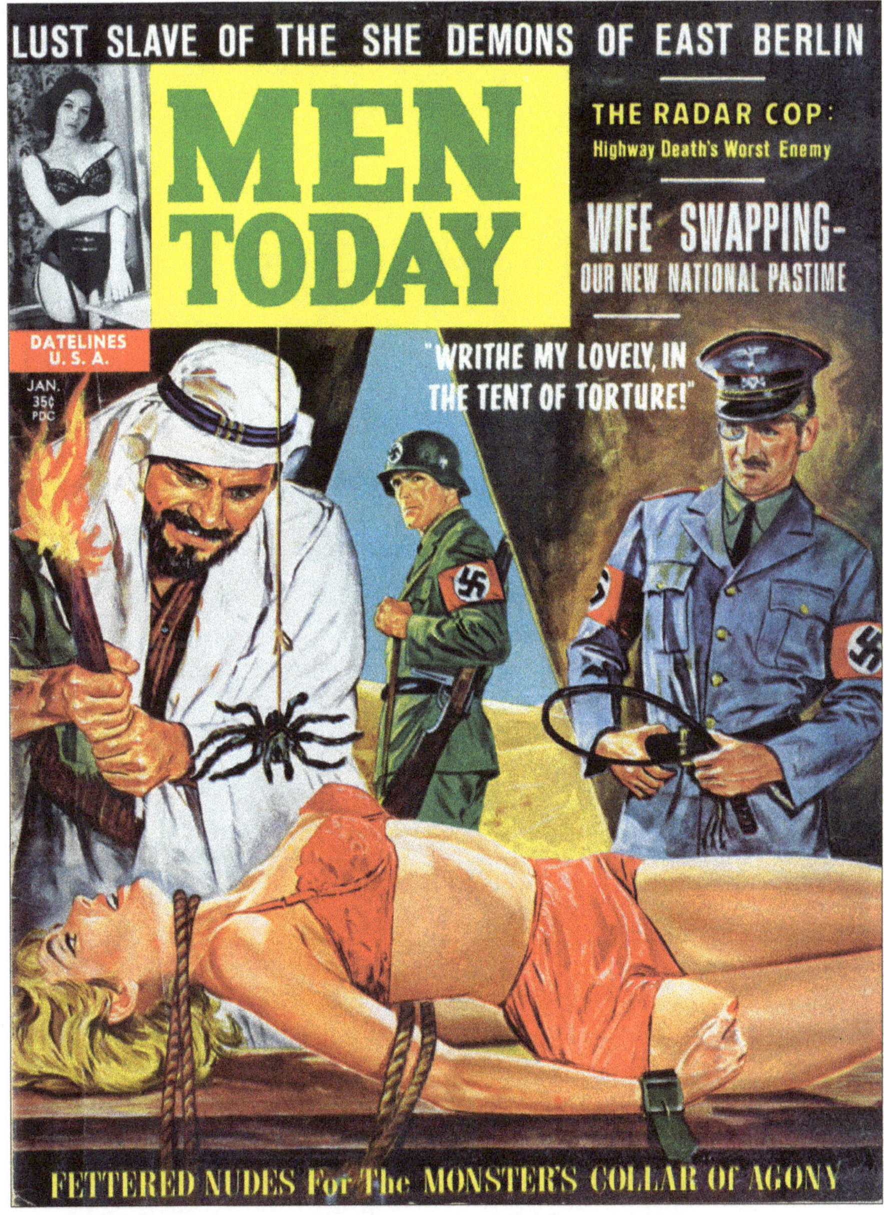

"Writhe My Lovely, in the Tent of Torture!" *Men Today* January 1963, art by Norm Eastman

"We Saved the Blonde Beauties From the Piranha Horror"
Man's Exploits June 1963, artist uncredited

The cover above has plenty to lure a MAM reader: near-naked damsels, a deadly snake, a snapping whip, and a trio of cruel tormentors in a bizarre torture scenario. But despite the story's title, what it does *not* have are piranha.

"Soft Maidens for the Monster's Devil Fish"

Men Today February 1963, art by Norm Eastman

(They're not both blondes, either.) Possibly the piece was originally created for a different use, then repurposed as a *Man's Exploits* cover. The Norm Eastman *Men Today* cover above, on the other hand, more than delivers.

Portfolio: CLARENCE DOORE

"EYES WIDE OPEN"

Champion For Men October 1959

"Barracudas Feasted on My Flesh" *Rage* June 1961

Clarence *Doore (1913-1988), one of the great artists who worked for men's adventure magazines, employed a very recognizable style. A Doore cover painting is easiest to ID when there's a damsel in distress in the scene; the big eyes and red, parted lips of Doore's women are a giveaway once you've seen a few. There's also* *a subtle feel of fantasy in his men's adventure magazine work, as opposed to the more photorealistic artwork of some other MAM illustrators.*

Doore got his start as an artist in 1937, doing interior and cover

Men in Conflict August 1962
(Artwork originally published as the cover of All Man *March 1959)*

illustrations for the magazine Open Road for Boys, *a competitor of* Boy's Life. *In the 1940s and early 1950s, he painted covers for classic pulp fiction magazines and comic books. Starting in 1950, he became one of the go-to*

All Man July 1959

Champion For Men September 1959   *Man's Exploits* November 1957

illustrators for the publishers of the emerging men's adventure magazine genre. In fact, he was one of the few artists who worked for almost all of the MAM publishers, rather than just a few.

Gusto December 1957   *Real Men* July 1958

"Coiled Death Vs. Mauling Murder" *Animal Life* July 1954

By the time he retired in 1966, Doore had created hundreds of cover and interior illustrations for a wide range of men's adventure magazines, including All Man, Animal Life, Battle Cry, Brave, Champion for Men, Courage, Escape to Adventure, For Men Only, Fury, Gusto, Male, Man's Adventure, Man's Daring, Man's Exploits, Man's Life, Man's Magazine, Man to Man, Men in Conflict, Rage for Men, Real Men, Rugged Men, Safari, Sir!, Spur, True Adventures, True Men Stories, *and* True Weird.

From 1964 to 1989, Robert F. Dorr (1939-2016) was a globe-hopping Foreign Service Officer for the US State Department. In his spare time, he wrote war and adventure stories for men's adventure magazines. He subsequently became a top military journalist and author of 80 military aviation and history books. We're partial to his somewhat different take on animal attack stories, as they tend to be sympathetic to the animals.

The same May 1973 issue of *Male* the following story comes from includes a second Dorr contribution, in an entirely different mode: "The Erotic Stewardess Tapes," a MAM "sexposé" *("Like most stewardesses, Kathy has an adventurous streak...")* featuring racy snaps by famed photographer Jerry Yulsman.

Bob's giant cougar story is also notable for being illustrated by Mort Künstler, under his pseudonym Emmett Kaye. Künstler did thousands of illustrations for magazines and books from the early 1950s to the 1980s. Since then, he has focused on creating historical paintings for high-end galleries and collectors. His Civil War paintings are especially sought after, often selling for tens of thousands of dollars.

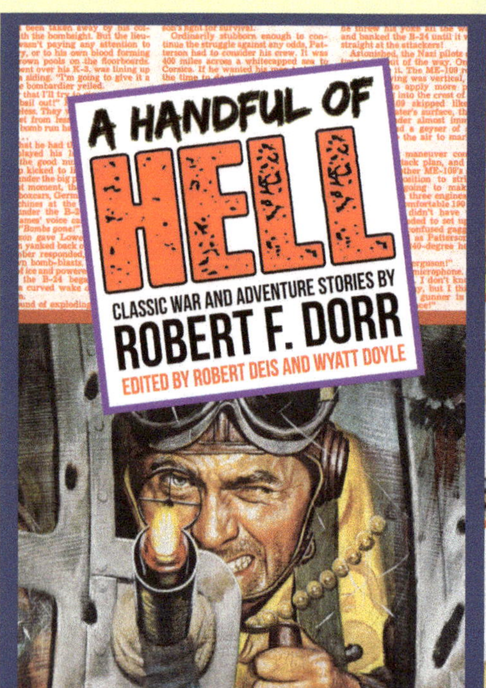

DELUXE HARDCOVER WITH ADDITIONAL CONTENT

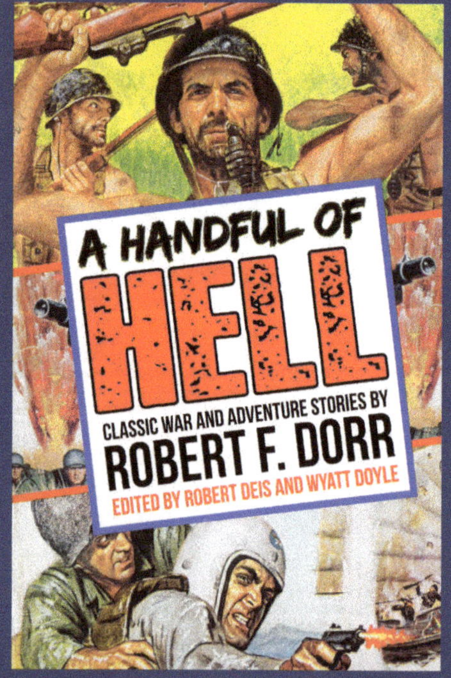

TRADE SOFTCOVER EDITION

The Men's Adventure Library release *A Handful of Hell* collects highlights from the early years of author, aviator and diplomat Robert F. Dorr. A prolific contributor to MAMs who went on to enjoy a long and celebrated career as a military historian and author of non-fiction, Dorr passed away in 2016.

"Strange Revenge of Wyoming's Most Hunted Giant Puma"

STORY BY ROBERT F. DORR

A Wounded Animal's Fur
AS the cat leaped, Irwin fired
in a desperate attempt to cut
down the beast in mid-air . .
TRUE
STRANGE
REVENGE OF
WYOMING'S
MOST HUNTED
GIANT PUMA
By PETE IRWIN
As told to
ROBERT F. DORR
ART BY EMMETT KAYE
EMMETT KAYE
16

...Vs. A 'Psycho' Tracker's Raw Hate

Normally, the big cat avoided humans. But a brutal game-poacher had painfully wounded the animal, which now ran berserk in a national forest, a threat to campers, woodsmen and fishermen...

WE were at the bottom of a V-shaped crevice and the mountain lion was advancing toward us along the skyline, remaining behind trees. I wasn't aware of the big cat until it stepped out from behind snow-covered aspens and looked down at us, its lean flanks quivering, its jaw open, the powerful teeth bared. The rugged Wyoming mountain lion has no real fear of any creature, including humans.

"Six hundred pounds, I'd say." My own voice sounded shaky. "Been studying us for a long time before moving in."

I stood at the bottom of that deep crevice in Wyoming's Medicine Bow National Forest with Lew and Nancy Carmichael, and at that moment in December of last year I had enough problems without a hungry mountain lion adding to them. I was studying the approaching cat when I should have been thinking about those problems, so I didn't notice when Lew clambered around and raised his rifle.

"No!" his wife screamed. "You can't!"

"You shut up!" Lew (Continued on page 76)

ART BY MORT KÜNSTLER (AS EMMETT KAYE)

We were at the bottom of a V-shaped crevice and the mountain lion was advancing toward us along the skyline, remaining behind trees. I wasn't aware of the big cat until it stepped out from behind snow-covered aspens and looked down at us, its lean flanks quivering, its jaw open, the powerful teeth bared. The rugged Wyoming mountain lion has no real fear of any creature, including humans.

"Six hundred pounds, I'd say." My own voice sounded shaky. "Been studying us for a long time before moving in."

I stood at the bottom of that deep crevice in Wyoming's Medicine Bow National Forest with Lew and Nancy Carmichael, and at that moment in December of last year I had enough problems without a hungry mountain lion adding to them. I was studying the approaching cat when I should have been thinking about those problems, so I didn't notice when Lew clambered around and raised his rifle.

"No!" his wife screamed. "You can't!"

"You shut up!" Lew snapped back. "This is my chance!"

"You damned well better not," I broke in. "No matter how hungry it is, that cat won't attack us. It's illegal to shoot them and also dangerous."

"You be quiet too, Irwin. You're just the hired help here."

He was only feet away. I sprang and hit him with arms outstretched, intending to bat the rifle downward.

But I was too late. Lew aimed and jerked his trigger.

Problems? You couldn't find more of them than I had at that moment. My name is Pete Irwin and I'm a bush pilot working out of Tie

Siding, Wyoming, in the mountainous southwestern part of that state, one of the least populated and most rugged areas of the US.

Moments ago I'd landed my ski-equipped Cessna 210 on a frozen creek bed in that crevice in Medicine Bow to repair a faulty generator. It hadn't been a planned landing, but it wasn't exactly an emergency, either. I could repair the renegade equipment in an hour. Before we'd gone down, I'd prudently radioed my position to Cheyenne airport sixty miles east.

It would have been a "no sweat" situation except for my passengers, who were as different as two married people can be and had been fighting constantly since I'd met them. Lew Carmichael was the owner of a West Coast trucking firm and had a spare-time kick about trips to the wilderness. He was a big man, irritable and rancorous. He also had a ruggedly handsome face and prided himself on his good looks: I'd seen him admiring his own features in a mirror.

Nancy, his wife, was at least twenty years younger, a tall platinum blonde with all the friendliness and congeniality he lacked. They'd hired me to fly them over Medicine Bow National Forest so they could shoot a "home movie" about Lew's favorite subject—wild animals—and they'd argued about it from the moment we'd climbed into the airplane.

It was my fault that Lew had a rifle. There are no old, bold pilots in the Wyoming hinterlands. You survive by being prepared. Even on a routine flight, I'd insisted that we come equipped for every possible contingency.

Now Lew's rifle shot, Nancy's scream, and the mountain lion's pain-crazed outcry surged in my ears.

My body fell across Lew's, my full weight of 180 pounds slamming down on top of the rifle's stock and knocking the weapon into the snow.

Lew took a half-step backward and for a moment we were leaning on each other, swaying. "You goddamn fool!" I shouted into his face. "You shot that animal for nothing!"

Forty feet uphill, looking down at us from a height advantage that would make it easy to pounce, the mountain lion wobbled shakily, a blemish of red expanding on its shoulder where the blood came oozing out.

Lew had bungled the shot. The beast regained its balance, its rapid breath forming clouds of condensation in the air. It shrank down into a hunched position, as if getting ready to jump us. Lew and I forgot our feud with each other and tensed.

The big cat lunged at us.

It was a snarling, flailing blur of motion, its massive jaws open as it came swarming down. One of its huge, claw-tipped forepaws, powerful enough to kill with a single blow, passed within inches of my face.

The bulk of the animal actually passed between Lew and myself and both of us sidestepped. We turned to see the creature hit the snow and roll.

There were dabs of red in the rut of snow where the mountain lion landed. It thrashed around, then picked itself up and went loping down along the bottom of the crevice.

The big cat started across the frozen creek bed, paused to study my airplane, then changed direction and began struggling uphill—abandoning us.

My heartbeat was pounding in my throat. I gasped for breath while I grabbed Lew by the scruff of his coat and pulled him toward me.

"Look at the way that animal is moving! You see the limp, the way it sinks a little too low on its left forepaw? You did that! You put a .30-caliber, fine-grain slug into that mountain lion's shoulder and now it's berserk with pain. It doesn't know what it's doing!"

"It's your fault, Irwin!" The two of us had been on first names, Lew and Pete, until now. "If you hadn't knocked my rifle away, I'd have killed that beast. Listen . . ."

"No. *You* listen! Normally a mountain lion won't attack a man, even when provoked. But thanks to you, that tormented creature almost killed us. And because of what you did, it won't hesitate now to go after the next human it sees."

"Please, can't we stop this?" interrupted Nancy. "I'm frightened! I'm scared sick and I want to go home!"

I looked down into her green eyes. "I'm taking you home. Soon as I fix the aircraft. And if your husband has any sense, we won't see him around this part of the country any time again, ever."

"You can't tell me what to do!" Lew protested. "You're not working for me anymore!"

"No. No, I'm not. Because I've got something much more important to do. I've got to get back to Tie Siding and organize some men to track down that poor animal and put it out of the misery you created. Because if I don't, that mountain lion will maim or kill some innocent person. *You* transformed that animal into a killer, Lew, and somebody may die because of it . . . ."

Tɪᴇ Siding, Wyoming—population 37 —was the kind of town where I could hide inside my own problems and escape those of the world.

I rent the upper floor of Jim Wade's general store, which, except for the gas station, is Tie Siding's only place of business. Jim lets me keep my Cessna 210 on the flat strip of land he owns behind the store. I like living in a small and private place, but when the apartment starts to creep in on me, or when I want a woman, there's a settlement of tourist motels and night spots a few miles away along Interstate 230. That's where travelers, including my air charter customers, stay while exploring Medicine Bow.

Jim Wade is a portly, topheavy man who waddles rather than walks and who knows the mountains and forests of Wyoming like the back of his hand. After I landed and Lew and Nancy Carmichael took off for their motel in their rented car, I sought Jim's advice about the wounded mountain lion. We sat over a couple of beers in the back of his store and he nodded, agreeing with me.

"It's a serious matter, Pete. A mountain lion with a severe bullet wound will do almost anything. There's a lot of hunters and campers in the Medicine Bow area now, despite the onset of winter. Your big cat is going to be looking for trouble, and it'll attack on sight."

"The temperature's supposed to start falling this afternoon. It could get down near zero tonight. It'll be risky going after that cat, Jim."

"Consider what may happen if we don't. Anyway, Pete, I think you should phone the Highway Patrol and have Carmichael charged with shooting an endangered species. Then let's get some of the boys together and go after that cat."

We agreed to use my plane. Jim Wade would recruit two other guys who were expert woodsmen and rifle shots—Mark Cullahan, who ran the gas station, and Little Knife George, a full-blooded Kayonote Indian who managed a motel up along the Interstate.

We would search for the mountain lion from the air and, if unsuccessful, would land at the frozen creek where I'd been before and start on foot from there. It was still early afternoon so we have five or six hours of daylight.

I worked on the Cessna 210 alone, scraping frost from the wing surfaces and checking the control wires for signs of freezing. I looked again at the generator I'd fixed earlier and something caught my eye: A connector socket beneath my panel had been sliced out from inside the aircraft. I'd repaired it without noticing that the damage was man-made. *Lew Carmichael had seen that mountain lion from the air and had purposely sabotaged my aircraft so I would have to land near it.*

Wᴴɪʟᴇ tinkering with my aircraft I turned the VHF radio dial to the Highway Patrol's frequency and heard police voices discussing a tragic incident:

A 19-year-old camper, Henry A. Hirschbrun, from Cheyenne, had been attacked by a mountain lion on a remote snow slope. The berserk cat had dived on him and chewed up his leg. The camper's parents and a park ranger had gotten him to the hospital in Trail Creek, just across the Colorado border, but he was comatose from loss of blood and was listed in "very serious" condition.

Listening to this, I knew I'd made a grave mistake by not reporting to the authorities that a wounded mountain lion was running wild in Medicine Bow National Forest. I got on the radio and talked up a storm. The Highway Patrol said it was sending a helicopter from Cheyenne which would join us to help with the hunt.

Jim, Mack and Little Knife arrived at the aircraft and we were getting ready to take off when another vehicle departed Tie Siding's narrow road and lurched through the snow toward us—the Carmichaels' rented Ford Torino.

Alone, Nancy Carmichael was trembling and sobbing. "He's gone crazy!" she moaned. "He's a sick person, Pete, and if you can't stop him . . ."

"Hold it. Hold it. What's going on?"

"After we got back to the motel, Lew and I had a big fight." She told it between sobs. "Lew said that mountain lion is a special thing to him. It's some kind of a symbol. He said he's got to kill the mountain lion, so he grabbed his rifle and some gear and took off after it."

"Nancy, that crevice where he shot the animal is *seventeen miles away!*"

"He's got a snowmobile! They rent them up at the motel, you know. He left an hour ago and said he wasn't coming back until he'd bagged the animal. He's sick, and I'm afraid he'll hurt himself!"

"Or somebody else."

"Lew isn't normal. I've known that all along, but it only came into sharp focus for me today. He has some kind of a fixation."

I just looked at her. "This doesn't make much sense."

"Hell, I'm his *wife* and it doesn't make much sense to me, either! I know this: As a child, Lew was bitten by a dog and had to undergo weeks of extremely painful rabies treatments before learning that he didn't have the disease. He travels all over the country hunting animals, sometimes pretending that he only wants to photograph them. He has to prove to himself that he's superior to every creature in the animal world."

Nancy asked to come along in the aircraft and it was impossible to refuse. In fact, I envied Lew for having a pretty wife who worried about him more than he deserved. I couldn't miss the bruise under her eye where he'd apparently bashed her before stomping out.

We took off in a gathering crosswind, climbed out over the ridgeline just north of Tie Siding, and headed into Medicine Bow. The plane handled roughly. A cold front was moving down toward us, bringing higher winds and snow that would eventually make flying impossible.

LATER, much later, when the whole matter of the wounded mountain lion was resolved and there was no going back to change any part of what happened, I talked with a zoologist for the park service. Between us, we were able to reconstruct the movements of the big cat with a good degree of accuracy.

After taking the bullet high in the shoulder and breaking off its inconclusive encounter with Lew and me, the mountain lion limped awkwardly along the frozen creek bed for a few hundred feet.

Then, in its tortured, disoriented condition, the puma started uphill, leaving behind clear tracks with splotches of blood every few yards.

The attack on Hirschbrun came about a half hour later. The 19-year-old camper picked up the cat's trail halfway up the slope and began following it out of curiosity.

After entering the treeline near the crest of the ridge and finding himself in a maze of aspens, Hirschbrun began to worry and broke off his pursuit. He was turning away, ready to hike back to his parents' camp nearby, when the mountain lion sprang at him from behind.

The mountain lion had attacked Hirschbrun out of a pain-crazed instinct that it was being threatened. When the boy lay incapacitated, the creature abandoned him just as rapidly as it had abandoned Lew and myself.

In early afternoon, the lion entered the region of Medicine Bow National Forest known to local residents as the "ice biscuit lakes"—small, round bodies of frozen water which are perfectly symmetrical and look as if they were dug out of the earth with a cookie cutter. Each time it stepped on ice, the animal tried to regain its bearings and choose a new route.

THOUGH it kept changing course and inscribing wide circles around the lakes, the mountain lion was moving in a consistent direction—toward high ground, a heavily-wooded area that was favored by woodsmen at this time of year. The animal was instinctively heading for cover.

Wedged against each other in the cold, cramped interior of my Cessna 210, we peered down intently while I cut the throttle and descended over the crevice where I'd landed earlier. Even before I spotted it, Jim Wade picked out the spot where we'd had our first encounter with the mountain lion. Further upstream, he discovered tracks heading uphill. But we lost the lion's path in the aspen trees and I had to climb again and begin circling. A radio message came in telling me that the police helicopter would join us shortly.

"But there's something else down here, too," said Jim.

"Huh?"

"Snowmobile tracks."

Much later, of course, it was also possible to reconstruct the movements of Lew Carmichael. Lew must have had a topographical map and some navigating skills, because he made remarkably good time, following carved-out creek beds, avoiding the ridge slopes, and taking only slightly more than an hour to cover 17 miles.

His fast vehicle easily traversed the ridge where Hirschbrun had been attacked.

Ignoring the frigid cold wind that penetrated his heavy clothing, Lew picked up the lion's trail once more among the "ice biscuit" lakes. Finally, less than half a mile from the high ground, Lew spotted a sluggishly moving amber shape ahead of him and realized he was within sight of the mountain lion.

The poor animal must have guessed it was being stalked. When Lew's vehicle appeared in a cloud of snow particles a thousand feet behind, the wounded cat suddenly veered sharply to the left and limped with remarkable speed toward the only cover in sight—tall, snow-laden trees.

Lew cursed as the creature vanished behind the treeline. The terrain was bumpy here and he had to juggle his controls to get the snowmobile to follow. He never realized that the mountain lion was using the cover of brush to double around behind him.

Suddenly, there was a low, growling sound and the big cat came bounding out of the trees. Lew turned to see the great bulk of the creature plummeting at him. He swayed involuntarily. The cat slammed into his vehicle and tipped it over on top of him.

Lew sprawled in the snow, his rifle out of reach. He saw the amber hide of the animal pass over him, an outstretched paw grazing his clothing.

Then the animal was circling again, several feet from him, and Lew discovered he couldn't move. The heavy steel frame of the snowmobile was lying across his legs.

He was too shocked to feel any pain, but a glance at his legs told him what he'd sensed already: Both of his legs were broken. He was flat in the snow, the chilling moisture seeping through his clothing, and he couldn't move.

He flapped his arms uselessly in the snow, cried out, and looked across open space at the mountain lion. The wounded creature just stood there, its massive head shaking from side to side, its breath forming clouds of vapor. The jaw was open, the teeth bared, and the huge animal was staring directly at Lew—recognizing him as its tormentor.

This confrontation between man and beast stood out in bold relief for the five of us in my Cessna as I held the aircraft steady, tracing Lew's snowmobile tracks.

"The guy's doing our work for us," said Little Knife George when I dipped the Cessna's wings and descended. "It's sad we have to kill the lion—and it's his fault—but if he does it, what the hell?"

We spotted them at the edge of the aspens, Lew pinned in the snow, the lion looking at him. Nancy Carmichael stiffened and the color drained from her face. We held a hasty discussion and decided that, because of the wind, it would be impossible to shoot the beast from the air. There was too much chance of hitting Lew.

Old, bold pilots have better sense than to attempt to land a loaded two-ton Cessna 210 on a frozen lake.

Still, there wasn't time to wait for the promised helicopter. Ignoring the risk, and my own principles as a pilot, I picked the only flat surface in sight—the large, round "biscuit" lake—and set up a landing pattern.

We hit the slick ice at a bad angle, bounced, and then settled. The Cessna caught the ice and I stood on the brakes. We halted and piled out of the aircraft, at least a quarter-mile from Lew.

Mack Cullahan stayed with the plane. Lugging rifles, Jim, Little Knife and I led the woman across open terrain toward the spot where Lew Carmichael still lay pinned flat, the mountain lion circling warily around him.

WE TRUDGED at a fast pace through powdery snow that clung to us, walking into a frigid wind that was gaining intensity. As we drew within eyesight, we saw the wounded cat jabbing at Lew with a paw, experimenting with him.

If the wounded, tormented animal were capable of feeling, it would have felt that it was enjoying a moment of revenge. The man lying

Male February 1976, art by Ted Rand

(Story by Walter Kaylin, credited to "Wesley Leggett as told to Roland Empey")

beneath the mountain lion was completely helpless. He squirmed and flailed, shouting out words that didn't make any sense, but he was unable to defend himself. The lion could crush him with its heavy paw or sink its teeth into him at any moment it wished.

But the lion did not attack. In the end, its inbred habit of not assaulting human beings was stronger than the maddening effect of its wound. The lion stood over Lew and toyed with him, ripping away fragments of his clothing, drawing blood, but not making the fatal strike.

I dropped to my knees, lined up the creature in my telescopic sight, trying for a long shot that would end its misery instantaneously.

"Wait!" Jim Wade cautioned. "It's too close to him!"

"You'll hit Lew!" Nancy cried, "Please, don't!"

Lew's voice carried to us, a panicked outcry of shock and terror that didn't need words.

"I can't wait. That cat may change its mind and dig into him any second."

Holding my breath, bracing the rifle heavily, I squeezed the trigger. The gunshot echoed around us. The mountain lion stiffened, twitched, and fell backward.

Moments later, while a police helicopter orbited overhead, we stood beside the carcass of the mountain lion, lifted the snowmobile from Lew's legs and raised him free. The chopper carried Lew and his wife to the hospital and the rest of us spent that afternoon cleaning everything up— burying the animal and salvaging Lew's vehicle. It was many weeks later when I received a short note from Nancy Carmichael on the West Coast telling me that her husband was recuperating from his physical injuries and had agreed to seek psychiatric help for his mental problems. The good looks he prided himself upon had been permanently scarred by the puma's claws.

A great, beautiful creature had died for no reason. Every once in a while, flying over Medicine Bow National Forest, I spot a mountain lion from the air and think about all the problems Lew caused. I hope he learned something, because there aren't many of the big cats left, and I'd like to see the rest of them survive. ●

Hunting Adventures Summer 1956, art by Rafael De Soto

Man's Magazine December 1956, art by Harry Schaare

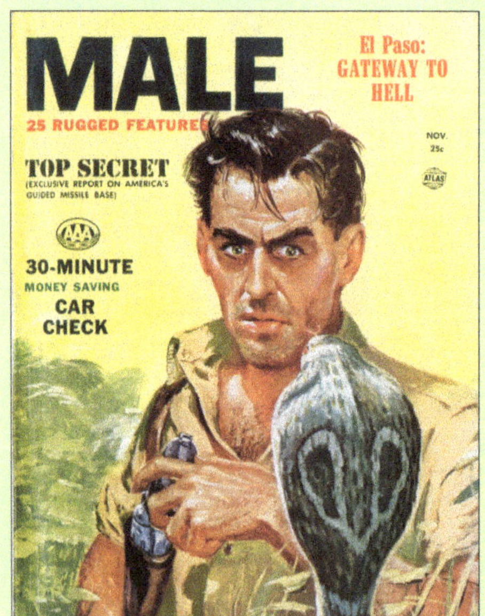

Male November 1952, art by Harvey Kidder

Man's Adventure July 1959, art by Clarence Doore

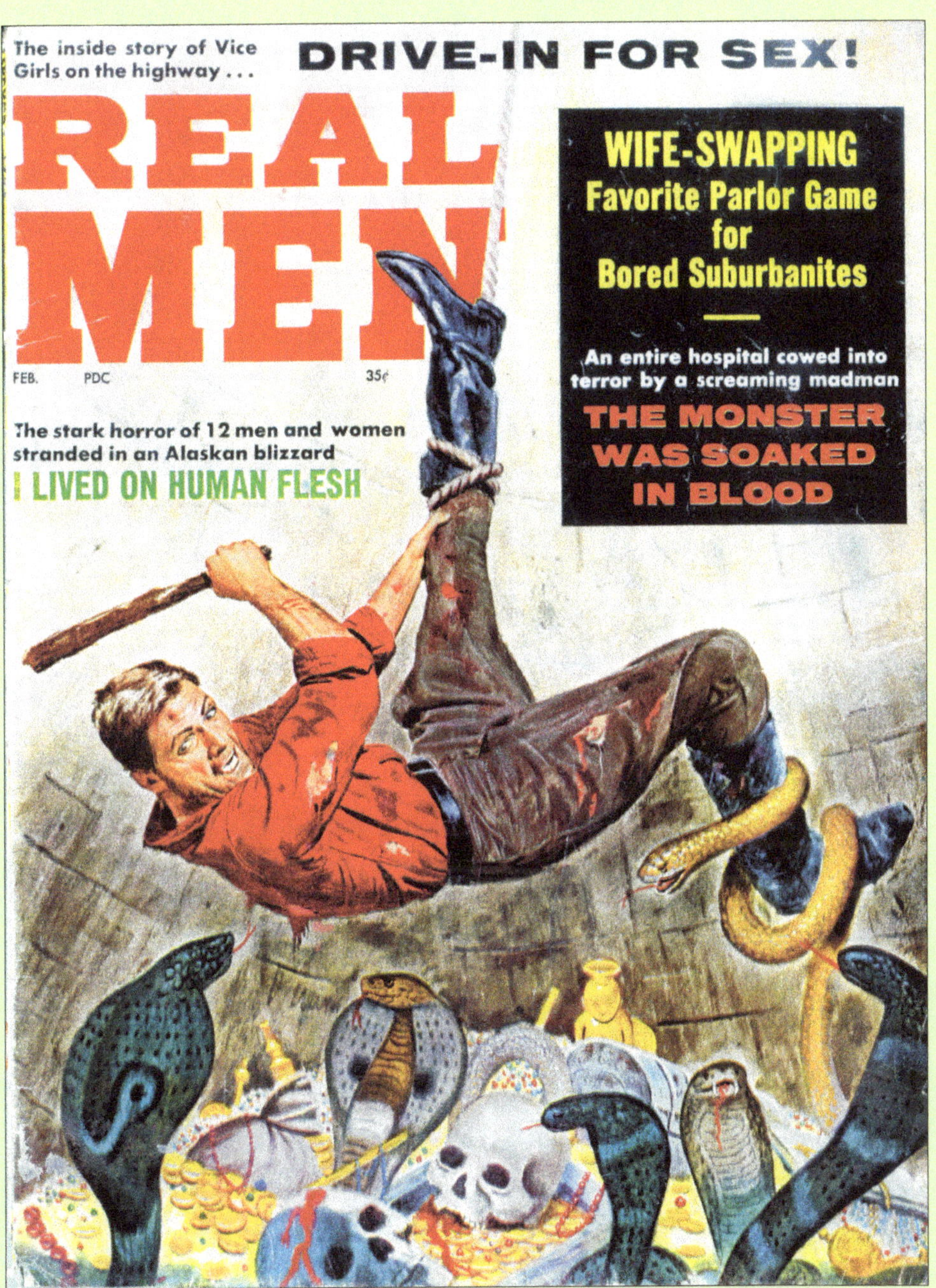

Real Men February 1962, artist uncredited
(*Artwork later reused as the cover of* Real Action *June 1964*)

on the page

Only once had a man come back, and he was mad.

No others returned, but men still looked for . . .

THE
TREASURE OF
PRITHVI RAJ

as told by Robert Gortz

LAND VALUATION was my business and this time it had got me to Government House in Karachi during the Pakistan boundary negotiations with India. While there I met Prince Prithvi Raj, one of India's minor maharajahs. The prince was a good friend to have, both socially and from a business angle.. After three months together in Karachi, we were old pals.

I was having a drink that night in Bill Denny's quarters. Bill was there as military attache and had known the Prince longer than I. There was a hammering on the door and Prithvi Raj marched in. He was still in lather-splashed polo kit, and he looked excited. He glanced around the room.

"Where is Bill Denny?" he asked.

"Bill's with Colonel Banjari," I said. "Anything wrong?"

He stood there, spring-cleaning me with his dark, piercing eyes. "There's no time to lose, Bob. I'm going to tell you something which will probably sound crazy and unbelievable, but I've got to give somebody the facts before I go."

"Shoot," I said.

He started pacing up and down the room, slapping his right fist into his left palm. I'd never seen him so excited.

"You know that centuries ago, when the Mogul Empire was falling apart, we held the Province of Mahdipur. You've heard of our lost treasure which was hidden when the Pathans defeated us and drove us out. That treasure consisted of gems worth several million rupees, and the clue to where it was hidden was lost when my ancestor was slaughtered on the battlefield.

"For three centuries," he said, "my family has searched for the clue without success. And now here—*here*—Bob, is the clue at last!"

I gaped at the piece of flimsy paper he thrust under my nose. Hindustani script was scrawled on it. "Are you trying to say that this is the clue to the Prithvi treasure?" (Continued on page 51)

ILLUSTRATED BY BOB WAGNER

"The Treasure of Prithvi Raj" *Outdoor Adventure* June 1957, art by Bob Wagner

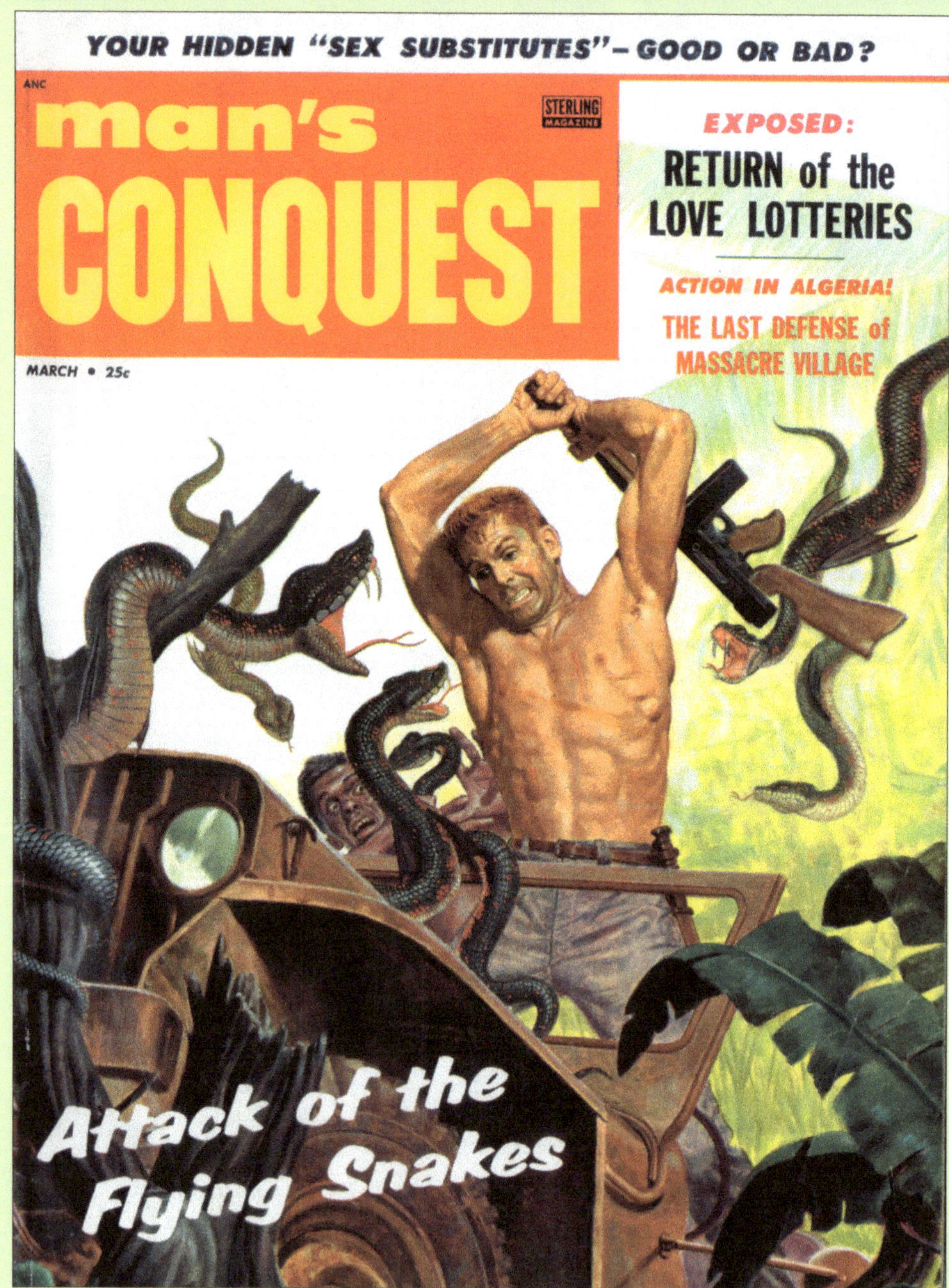

 "Attack of the Flying Snakes" *Man's Conquest* March 1957, art by T. Harris

Men February 1955,
art by Rafael DeSoto

Cavalcade January 1959,
art by Rafael DeSoto

A-OK for Men October 1962,
art by Rafael DeSoto

In a field notorious for over-the-top violence and excess, one prolific MAM writer was regularly singled out by his peers as a master of turning it up to eleven: Walter Kaylin (1921-2017).

Walter's first published stories were humorous pieces for *The Saturday Evening Post*. He also published two novels. But his primary legacy is as a writer of ripping yarns for men's adventure magazines. From the mid-1950s to the mid-1970s, Walter produced hundreds of them for the iconic Atlas/Diamond group of MAMs published by Martin Goodman's Magazine Management Company, including *Action for Men, For Men Only, Male, Man's World, Men*, and *Stag*. He was a favorite of other notable writers at Magazine Management, such as novelist/playwright/screenwriter Bruce Jay Friedman and Mario Puzo, author of *The Godfather*. In a talk with Josh Alan Friedman reprinted in our *Weasels Ripped My Flesh!* anthology, Puzo remembered: *"(Kaylin) was outrageous, he just carried it off."*

Kaylin's style of literary brinkmanship was ideally suited to MAMs, and his contributions span all three decades of the genre's existence. His stories were sometimes attributed to pseudonyms like "Roland Empey" and "David Mars" to camouflage multiple Kaylin appearances in the same issue.

It's Roland Empey who's credited with authorship

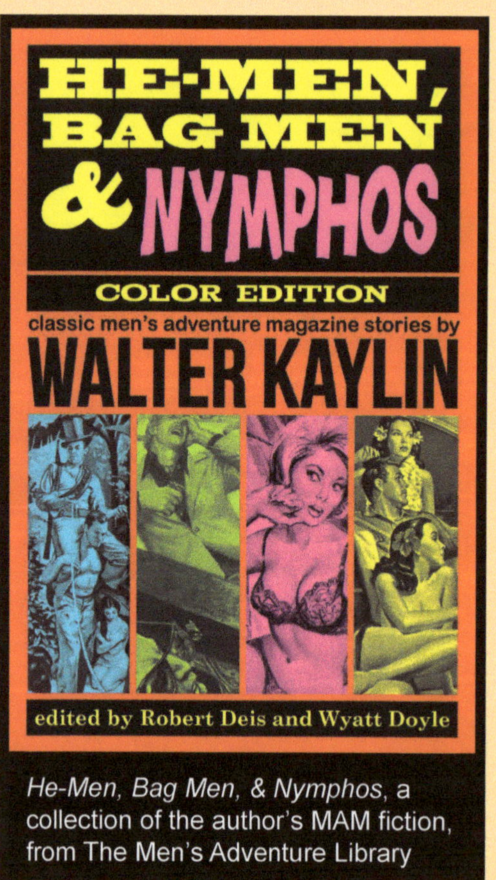

He-Men, Bag Men, & Nymphos, a collection of the author's MAM fiction, from The Men's Adventure Library

of "Trapped in the Bayou's Pit of a Million Snakes," but the story is unmistakably Kaylin. If "man vs. snake" was boilerplate MAM fiction, leave it to Kaylin/"Empey" to kick it up to a *million* snakes for this claustrophobic, hard-boiled squirmer. After all, why stop at a mere snake attack if there's an opportunity for a full-tilt snake *siege?*

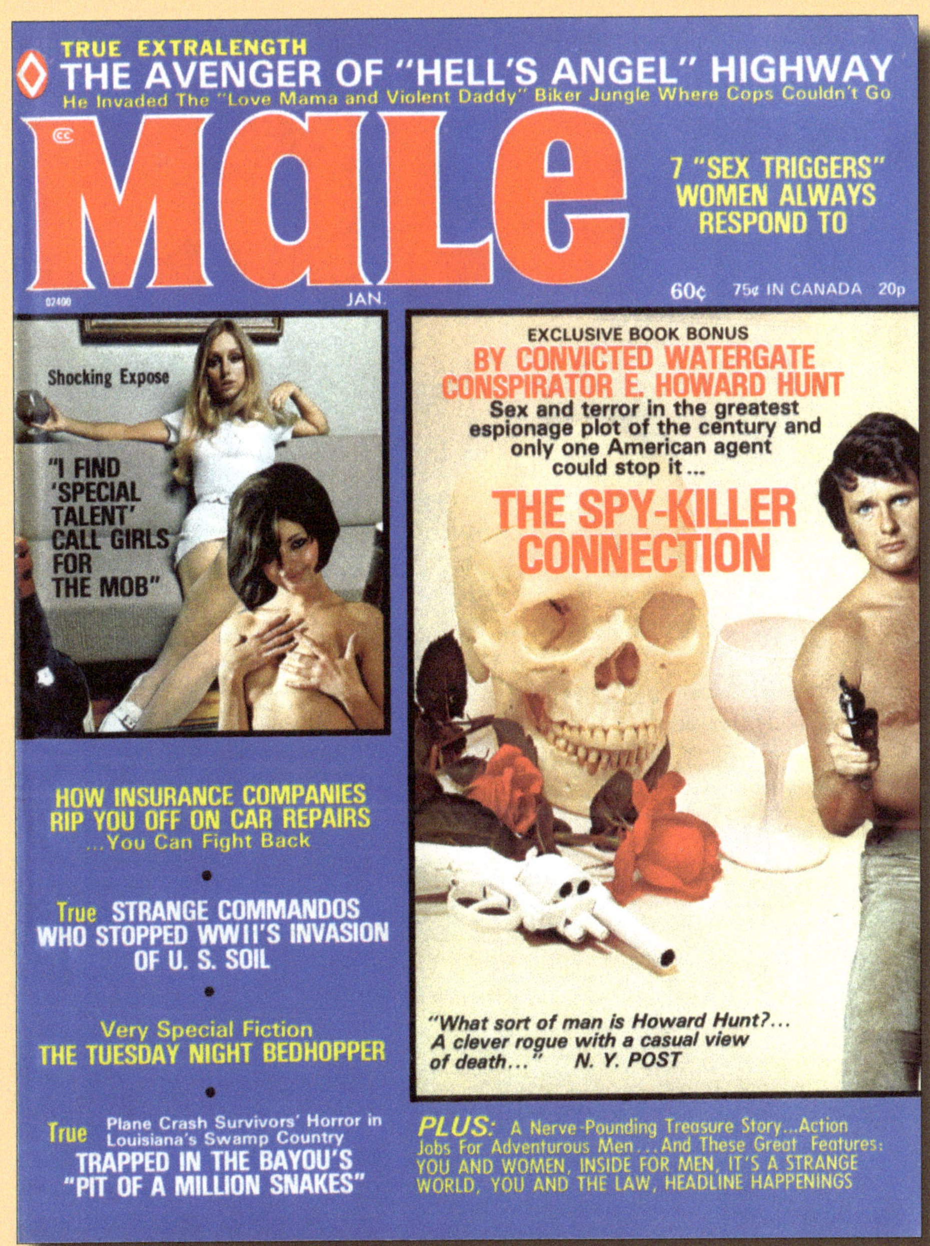

"Trapped in the Bayou's Pit of a Million Snakes"

STORY BY WALTER KAYLIN

PIT OF A MILLION SNAKES

By BEN TOLLIVER

as told to

ROLAND EMPEY

THE first one came down through a crack in the ceiling right above the instrument panel. It came down reaching around with its head and with the brown bands flowing in behind it, slick and slimy. The mouth was open and you saw the white inside it that gave the deadly reptile its name—cottonmouth.

I reached for Howard's collar where he sat in the pilot's seat and yanked him backward, dumping him on the floor. He shouted, "What the hell, Tolliver . . ." and ended it in a gurgle when he saw the snake drop, hit the panel and land in the seat he had just vacated.

Baylor laughed and said, "Let this old country boy show you how to handle him." He advanced an open hand toward where the snake was writhing around on Howard's leather seat cushion. He moved the hand slowly. His bald head, scarred from a broken-bottle fight with another con just a month earlier, was suddenly wet with sweat. His mouth was open and you saw a lot of purple gum broken up by a few jagged, tobacco-stained teeth.

We were awfully (Continued on page 58)

16

AS Tolliver shot the snake that had dropped onto the pilot's seat, Baylor hammered furiously at a second snake

17

ART BY BOB LARKIN

The first one came down through a crack in the ceiling right above the instrument panel. It came down reaching around with its head and with the brown bands flowing in behind it, slick and slimy. The mouth was open and you saw the white inside it that gave the deadly reptile its name—cottonmouth.

I reached for Howard's collar where he sat in the pilot's seat and yanked him backward, dumping him on the floor. He shouted, "What the hell, Tolliver . . ." and ended it in a gurgle when he saw the snake drop, hit the panel and land in the seat he had just vacated.

Baylor laughed and said, "Let this old country boy show you how to handle him." He advanced an open hand toward where the snake was writhing around on Howard's leather seat cushion. He moved the hand slowly. His bald head, scarred from a broken-bottle fight with another con just a month earlier, was suddenly wet with sweat. His mouth was open and you saw a lot of purple gum broken up by a few jagged, tobacco-stained teeth.

We were awfully quiet. Marty Howard was in a state of shock at what had almost happened to him. Baylor was concentrating so hard you could almost hear a whirring going on in his skull. And as the man in charge, I was wondering just what in hell my responsibilities were in this particular situation. Where would I stand if Baylor got bitten? Where would I stand if he died?

"Ahh!" That was Baylor. The snake had gone for his hand and he'd gotten it out of the way in time, then brought the other hand down behind its head and grabbed it up off the seat. All in one motion, he smashed the snake's head against a wall of the cabin, then dropped it to the floor and crushed the head under his heel. "Pretty smart for a country boy, isn't it?" he said and opened the plane's door.

I said, "Don't get nervous, Tolliver, don't get nervous. I'm just getting rid of this thing so it don't draw flies."

He threw the dead snake out and closed the door. I said, "That's not going to look too bad on your record, Baylor. You didn't do yourself any damage getting that thing out of here."

He laughed and said, "I don't know that that's going to make a hell of a lot of difference." The laugh was a high-pitched cackle. It did something to you at the base of your spine and the back of your neck.

I said, "What do you mean?"

He said, "Here, take a look," and opened the door again.

The mist lay over the ground like a tattered blanket, and at first I couldn't see through it. Then I saw movement under there and all of a sudden it was in focus, and that's when I thought I was going to be sick. There were thousands of them, their obscene bodies forming strange knots and tangles, wriggling, writhing, contorting, the white mouths of many of them opened wide.

Baylor said, "A plane coming down on them this way, most time they'd just crawl away. But we're in their nesting area, and they're going to stay."

I said, "That one getting in here was a freak thing, though, wasn't it? There don't figure to be . . ."

He laughed again, but the sweat all over his face was from fear. He said, "Stop fooling yourself, Tolliver. There are a million ways they can get in here, and they're going to use them all."

IT HAD started about two hours earlier. We didn't like the way some of the cons were acting at Pardee Farm, and it had been decided to relocate a couple of them. That's the modern idea, and Dave Wilson, the warden at Pardee, was all for doing things right. In the old days, you'd clout them around when they started that behind-the-back-of-their-hands whispering. You thought they might be planning a break and you wanted to knock that idea out of their heads before it got too far along. But the modern idea is to separate the potential troublemakers, and that's what we were doing with Buddy Baylor—moving him to Rutland Farm, 200 miles further down toward the Louisiana Gulf Coast.

Buddy—a happy kid's name. But Baylor was no happy kid. He was past 40. He'd spent pretty near half his life in the swamp jails of Louisiana and Mississippi for killing his wife and her lover with an axe, and if you ever took that laugh of his for him being happy, you'd be making a mistake. Baylor wasn't happy. Baylor was a little nuts.

Well, we moved him down by commercial plane. Of course, the State paid the tab. The plane was a three-seater owned by a swamp pilot named Marty Howard. Howard's main business was flying trappers and sportsmen in and out of the bayous, but he was available for prison work whenever we needed him. His only concern was that the con he was transporting didn't get rambunctious while the plane was in the air. We assured him there was no likelihood of that happening with Baylor. Baylor might have been a little nuts, but he was shrewd, too. Baylor knew I'd be sitting behind him ready to lay that big horse pistol alongside his head if he gave me any reason to do it. I was the head of the guards at Pardee, and I wasn't about to let a con make a fool out of me. I hadn't gotten up there that way.

The trip should have taken only an hour. Even with the mist filling the bayous like cotton batting, we should have done it in less than two. But somewhere along the line we started losing gas, losing it fast, and pretty soon Howard was looking for a place to put the plane down and cursing about a loose gas cap.

"That's all it could be, damn it, a loose cap. I know we don't have a leak." He was circling around, trying to find an opening through the mist-shrouded trees. "We're right in the neighborhood of a drop station," he said. "The closer I get us to it, the better." By a drop station, he meant a wooden shack on a block of cement where gasoline was stored to help out in emergencies like ours, and others where there were boats involved. He was quiet for a few minutes after that, and then he said, "All right, this ought to do it," and a minute later we came pancaking down in the swamp.

Howard blew his breath out. It was a sigh of relief. He hadn't been all that sure we were going to make it. He said, "All right, we're in okay shape now. We're close enough to the drop station to walk up there and get some more gas. We'll put it in and I'll see that the cap's on right this time. We can't take off right from here. The ground's too soggy for that. I can tell. It'll stop us from lifting off. But we're close to higher, harder ground and with some gas in the tank, we can taxi up there and then take off. No problem, no problem."

No problem? Well, of course, it didn't work out that way. He bent over his control panel, checking something out. Baylor and I watched him. I was deciding it would be Baylor and me that went for the gas. And then the cottonmouth came through the ceiling, aiming for the back of Howard's neck, and I yanked him out from under it just before it dropped. Baylor killed it, using a technique I wouldn't try if you put a gun to my head and ordered me to do it. But after he'd done it, where were we? I complimented him on what he'd done. I told him I'd enter it on his record and maybe it would help him later on. But he laughed in that crazy way of his and showed me that wriggling, writhing carpet of cottonmouths outside the plane. "We're in their nesting area," he said, "and they're going to stay. There are a million ways they can get in here and they're going to use them all."

We armed ourselves with wrenches and hammers. I wasn't going to use the pistol unless I had to. I didn't want to take a chance of putting a hole in the plane. I didn't think twice about whether or not to let Baylor have a hammer. We were going to need him. We were going to need Howard, too, but I didn't know if we had him. Howard was on the edge of hysteria. Pumas, tigers, anything else, he'd have probably been okay. But snakes do something to some people. They turn your blood to water. They turn your legs to straw. That's what was happening to Howard.

"There's one of the sons of bitches."

A WHITE mouth was coming up through a crack in the floor, the fangs extended. I jumped at it, stomping like a madman. My boot heel caught it just right and broke its head open, popping it like a sack of black filth. Incredibly, its body continued on into the plane, coiling up behind the crushed head and writhing all over the floor of the cabin. I tasted vomit in my mouth and swallowed it down. Baylor said from somewhere beside me, "Watch yourself jumping at them that way, Tolliver. They just might reach around and get you in the ankle."

Howard sobbed, "Oh, my God, here comes another one!" He was dancing, jigging to keep out of the dead one's way. And he was wrong

For Men Only January 1956, art by Clarence Doore

about it being another one. It was another two, another four, another seven, then even more. They were pouring in on us from cracks and holes all over the plane. Baylor and I were working pretty well, cracking away at them with our hammers and wrenches, but I had to curse Howard and backhand him across the face to get him into it. "Come on, damn it! We don't have time for that whimpering. Start hitting, start hitting!" He got into it then, but was still shrinking back, and there wasn't an awful lot he could get done that way.

"We can't keep it up much longer."

That was Baylor shouting in my ear. He wasn't laughing any more.

He was twitching around the mouth. His eyes were glassy. I shouted back, "What the hell else can we do?"

He said, "We need that gas. We've got to get out of here. Someone has to go for it."

I started to say something and he waved his hammer at the window. "Look there."

Between taking raps at those evil, darting heads, I sneaked a quick look where he was pointing. A big alligator was lumbering out of the mists straight toward the plane. Its mouth was open. What looked to be long strands of spaghetti were hanging down over its jaw. But, of course, it wasn't anything as innocent as that. It was cottonmouths— one monster devouring others. Baylor shouted, "He'll eat them by the hundreds. They're always doing it. The snakes know it. They'll try to get out of his way. I could make a run for it . . ."

I BROKE in on him. "Not you, Baylor. You're the con. I'm the guard. We don't do it that way."

His eyes were wild. "One, two bites and you're dead, Tolliver. With me, I could take a lot more. I come from the bayous. I've had it happen before. I can take more of them than you. I've got some immunity to the venom."

I said, "We don't do it that way, Baylor. I'll make the run."

It wasn't the kind of thing you think too long about. You want to move before you've got time to change your mind. I got Howard to tell me where the drop station was, which way to head. Then Baylor yanked the door open and I jumped out, not looking, just jumping, jumping out into whatever it was going to be like out there. Right into the heavy *shhhhhhh*. The sickening stink. The jabbing heads. The white mouths unhinging. And then I was into them up to the ankles with the big 'gator no more than 15 feet away and shoving his snout into them, feasting on them.

I started running. My mind was spinning with the horror of my situation. I was sloshing through snakes, kicking my way through them, swinging my head like a rearing horse so I wouldn't have to see. Then pain in both legs, sharp, tearing pain. And then I was stumbling, falling, screaming in sheer, blind terror as I felt the crush of their wriggling bodies all about me. *Would I drown in them? Good God! Would I go down and be buried alive? Could there be a greater ordeal, a worse way of dying?*

"Kick your legs, Tolliver. Kick your legs, man, kick your legs."

Baylor's voice. He was pulling me to my feet. He was dragging me back to the plane. His hand was an iron claw under my arm and I was sobbing, sobbing like a baby. We reached the door. I saw Howard's white face above me. He reached down to take me. Baylor pushed. They had me in. Baylor barked, "Knock them back, Howard. Knock them back the best way you can. It's more important that I do this."

He was yanking at my boots and socks, pushing my trouser legs up. I had a vague, shadowy sense of Howard swinging a hammer like a maniac. Was I dying or only fainting? Everything was blurred and shifting in front of me. Then Baylor rose up before me, glistening in sweat and menacing me with a knife. He rose and fell toward me and I felt his knife digging into my legs and feet and then his mouth was there, sucking, spitting, sucking the poison out of me and spitting it out.

Then he rose again. "This ain't no thing about cons and guards any more, Tolliver," he said. "This is just surviving. I got a lot of their poison out of you, but some will pump right into your heart if you excite yourself. So don't try stopping me, Tolliver. You're dead if you do."

He had the door open again. He had the knife in one hand and nothing at all in the other. I said, "Baylor," but it came out as a sort of weak gasp and he jumped out without even looking back.

I heard Howard mutter, "The ugliness of it, it's more than you can take in—the snakes, the 'gator . . ."

I sat up. I could see Baylor swinging his arm back and forth, slashing with the knife, moving away from the plane. He disappeared suddenly, lunging into the mists.

HOWARD said, "I'm sorry about crapping out on you back there, Ben. I'm all right now. Maybe that big 'gator taking the pressure off is helping."

The floor of the plane was covered with dead snakes, some of them still moving. But no more were coming in. The 'gator was right up against the plane outside, bumping it with his heavy body. You could hear the awful sounds of him gorging himself and the endless *shhhhhhhh* of the snakes.

I'd been lying on the floor of the plane, right in there with the dead snakes. That's where Baylor had "doctored" me. I sat up now. My voice

came out in a whisper. "I couldn't stop him from going. I was too weak.
They'll say I screwed up everything back at Pardee. It will cost me my
job, my reputation. Even if we don't get out, everyone will know what
happened and laugh at me for it. I got myself snake-bit and let a con get
away."

Howard wasn't listening to me. He was muttering, "By God, we
could do it now. If we had a teaspoonful of gas, just enough to taxi
us . . ." He was in the door of the plane, looking out. I dragged myself to
my feet and came up behind him, stepping on dead snakes. The plane ran
yellow and black with their insides, and it stank in a sickening way I can't
even begin to describe. I looked out over Howard's shoulder. The 'gator's
snout was half covered with snakes. He was rooting in them, throwing
his head back so they would slide down his throat, swallowing them
whole. Further on, you saw nothing but mists with the shadowy outlines
of trees somewhere in there.

I said, "Don't tell me I'm seeing what I'm seeing."

A figure was stumbling toward us. One hand was swinging
downward at the ground. You saw a knife in that hand. You saw a five-
gallon can of gasoline in the other. You heard a scream, a howl. Howard
muttered, "The poor bastard."

Baylor reached the wing of the plane. The gas tank was there. He
had snakes on both legs. One was biting at him just below one knee and
the other just above the other knee. He howled in awful pain, brushed at
them with a hand, then got himself up to the gas tank. He unscrewed the
cap and started to pour the gasoline. The snakes were coiling around his
legs and biting at him all the while. We could hear him grunting, panting.
At last he flung the can away and closed the gas tank. His hands went
to his legs. They each came off with a snake. He smashed their jabbing
heads together, smashed them again and again, maybe losing his mind.
Then lurching, staggering, he came toward the plane and we pulled
him in.

"Thought I was going to take off, didn't you, Tolliver?" He fell to the
floor like a sack of old clothes. His trousers were ripped to shreds where
the snakes had bitten him. His face was a mass of tics and twitches. Saliva
dribbled out of both corners of his mouth and his eyes were fastened on
mine, yet didn't seem to see me. "Thought I was going to take off . . ."

THERE was nothing to it after that. We taxied out of that soggy ground, rolling over hissing snakes and past the big 'gator still gorging himself on them. We reached the drop, which was up on higher, drier ground, and filled our tanks the rest of the way there. A few minutes later, we were in the air and completing our trip to Rutland.

They put both Baylor and me in the infirmary there. I was sick, but not too bad off because Baylor had sucked most of the poison out of my system. He was in terrible shape though, raving and screaming and absolutely out of his mind for three straight days. He began settling down after that, but it was another five days before I was able to see him. He lay on a cot looking thin and pale and with his glassy eyes staring at me from where I came walking in till I reached his bed. The scars stood up on his head as though they'd been engraved there. His voice was so weak, I had to put my ear to his mouth to hear him.

"What are you going to do for me, Tolliver?"

I said, "What do you mean, Baylor?"

I could see a vein pulsing in his head. It looked like it was going to pop. He got a hand on my wrist, digging the nails in. "I want out, Tolliver. I want a pardon. I want a pardon for saving your life. That's true, ain't it, Tolliver. I saved your life, didn't I? Didn't I? Didn't I?" His voice was rising, becoming a scream. "I did, didn't I? Didn't I save your life, Tolliver?"

I worked my hand free and left him. He was raving. There was no point in staying. He screamed and cursed at me all the way to the door.

He's calmed down by now. He's the old Baylor again. After all, this was some months ago. I've filled out the papers starting the ball rolling on getting him a pardon, but I know they'll never go through. They've got him on the books as crazy. They've got him down for having killed two people with an axe. They're not about to set old Baylor free. No, no, not a chance of that.

In a way, I can understand it. You don't want a man like Baylor running around loose. But there's this, too, there's got to be this. It's going to be tough on me seeing him so often in the years that lie ahead. It's going to be tough having him looking at me—not saying anything, just looking—both of us knowing how It was that day in the bayou.

Yeah, that's going to be tough. ●

True War January 1958, art by Mal Singer

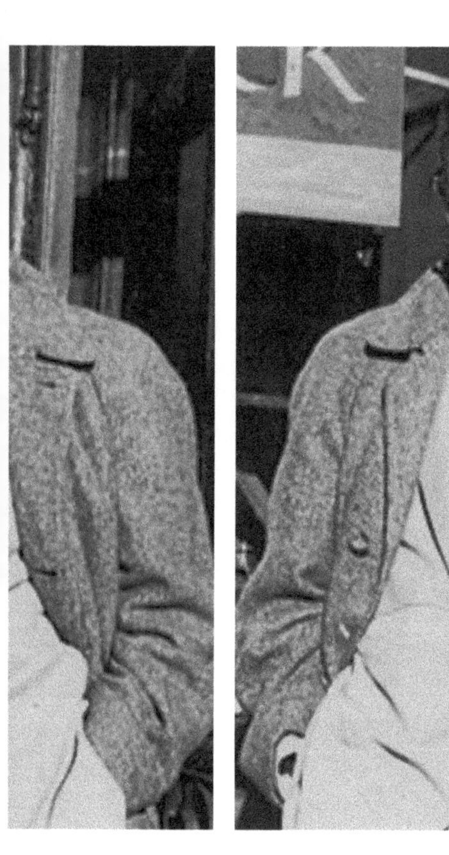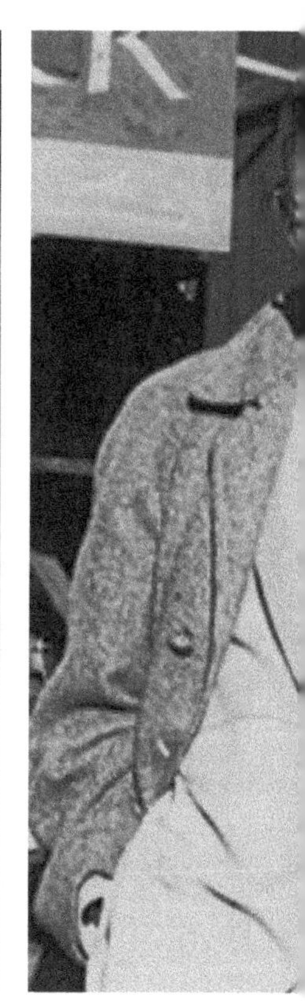

for
Walter Kaylin
1921–2017

Shark-themed pulp fiction and illustration art! Each action-packed tale is paired with commentary and mythbusting by a panel of celebrated contemporary shark experts.

There's never been a book like it.

MensPulpMags.com

new texture

Atomic Werewolves and Man-Eating Plants: When MAMs Got Weird

Featuring Theodore Sturgeon, Manly Wade Wellman, Gardner Francis Fox, Gil Paust, Rick Rubin *and more*

MAM stories of supernatural encounters, monstrous cryptids, vampirism, witchcraft, demonic death cults, killer robots, and of course, atomic werewolves and man-eating plants!

Recommended by The Washington Post

A Handful of Hell
Stories by Robert F. Dorr

Aviator, diplomat, and historian, Robert F. Dorr was uniquely qualified to write for men's adventure magazines, bringing sweat-and-blood, nuts-and-bolts authenticity to his stories of risk, combat, and sacrifice. Vivid, gripping tales of aerial conflict, battlefield heroism and action—some fact, some fiction, all adrenaline-fueled, white-knuckle adventure from one of the genre's greatest voices.

Barbarians on Bikes
Afterword by Paul Bishop

An oversized color collection compiling three decades of motorcycle-themed magazine covers and interior spreads from the 1950s through the 1970s, most unseen since their original publication. Biker illustration art at its most savage. A biker movie between covers, **Barbarians on Bikes** is big, bad, and untamed… Think you can handle the ride?

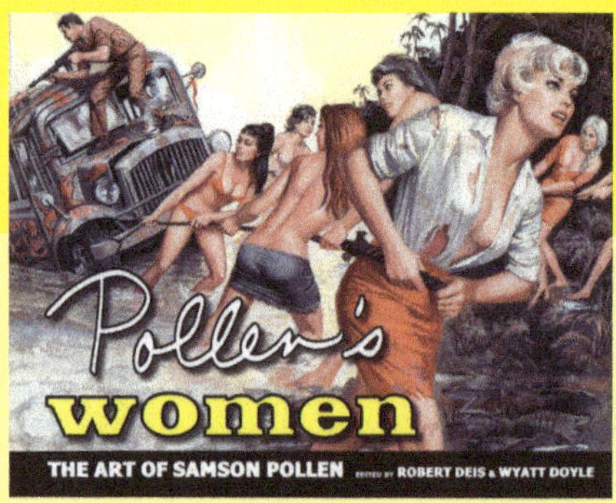

THE ART OF SAMSON POLLEN
Pollen's Women
Pollen's Action
Pollen in Print 1955–1959

A series of lush visual archives collecting some of artist Samson Pollen's most memorable pieces, selected from the hundreds of jaw-dropping illustrations he provided for men's adventure magazines (MAMs) from the 1950s through the 1970s. Pollen was equally celebrated for his abilities to effectively render action and movement, as well as his gift for painting beautiful and dangerous women. Illustrating work from authors like Mario Puzo, Martin Cruz Smith, Richard Stark (Donald Westlake), Norman Mailer, Ed McBain, Richard Wright, Don Pendleton, Erskine Caldwell, Walter Kaylin, and Robert F. Dorr, Pollen's immersive illustrations transported adventure-hungry readers from tropical jungles to brutal battlefields to raging seas and mean city streets. Samson Pollen painted it all—spectacularly. Yet almost none of these stunning illustrations have seen print since their original publication. Until now.

Both **Pollen's Women** and **Pollen's Action** are drawn from the artist's own exhaustive archives of his original artwork for MAMs, while **Pollen in Print 1955–1959** is the inaugural volume of a projected series presenting his artwork chronologically as it appeared in the magazines, allowing us to fill gaps in Pollen's archive and definitively chart the trajectory of a remarkable career.

All three big 11" x 8.5" horizontal volumes include the late artist's reminiscences and autobiographical comments.

Eva: Men's Adventure Supermodel
by Eva Lynd

Blonde Swedish countess Eva Lynd's multi-faceted career touches every aspect of 20th century popular culture. A model for leading illustration artists and top glamour and pin-up photographers of the era, she also appeared with some of the biggest names in entertainment on both the big and small screens. Eva shares her story in her own words and pictures. Includes artwork from pulp masters such as Norm Eastman, Al Rossi, Mike Ludlow, and James Bama.

One Man Army *by* Gil Cohen

Exploring the incomparable talent of Gil Cohen via the unique perspective he brought to the Mack Bolan universe as one of **The Executioner** series' most celebrated cover artists. **One Man Army** showcases Cohen's spectacular and original paintings for the bestselling action paperbacks, chronicling his seminal role in establishing the Bolan mythos for millions of dedicated readers worldwide.

Mort Künstler: The Godfather of Pulp Fiction Illustrators

Celebrated for his ability to present large-scale action while never losing sight of essential details, **Mort Künstler** is a master of capturing conflict in paint—both its spectacle, and human cost. At last, here is a stunning selection of his finest pieces from the MAM era in this long awaited collection. A close study of an unequaled career, every page explodes with action, color, and artistry.

Exotic Adventures of Robert Silverberg

From safari to bordello, from smugglers' cove to opium den, Robert Silverberg's lost pulp exotica returns to print for the first time since its original 1950s publication, presented in bold new facsimile re-creations that look fresh off the newsstand, circa 1958. Strap in for fully illustrated globe-trotting adventures from the vivid imagination of one of speculative fiction's most honored talents, working incognito.

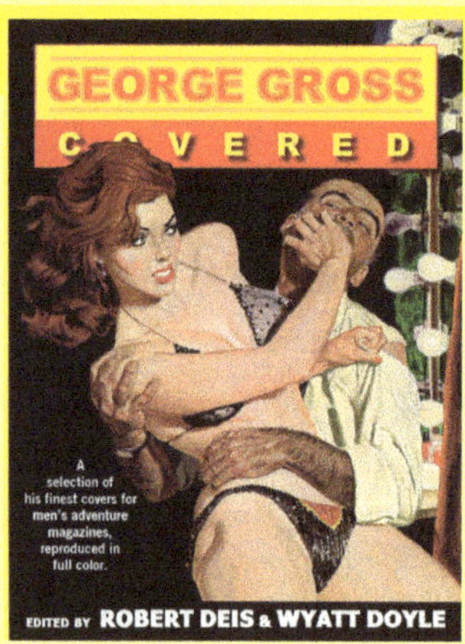

George Gross: Covered

A top artist for pulps, men's adventure magazines, and paperback covers, George Gross's artwork spans decades, and helped establish a visual vocabulary for action/adventure and hard-boiled fiction. A unique talent who led the way for generations of artists, his imagery continues to inspire and influence. Spotlighting dozens of his memorable covers, this full-color collection includes contributions by historian David Saunders and artist Mort Künstler.

The Naked and the Deadly
Stories by Lawrence Block

Spicy detective stories, international intrigue, and bedroom secrets… Before the bestsellers, Block cut his teeth on MAM fiction and nonfiction articles, collected here in their complete and uncut versions for the first time since their original publication. Includes a new introduction by the author.

Black Cracker, *an autobiographical novel by* Josh Alan Friedman

1962, flashpoint of the civil rights struggle. And young Josh is the lone white boy in a segregated grade school. An unflinching fun-house tour of a Long Island boyhood, and its now-forgotten poor Black shantytowns. Hilarious and heartbreaking.

Tell the Truth Until They Bleed, *by* Josh Alan Friedman

Up close and personal with important and unsung figures in blues and rock 'n' roll: the self-made, the self-serving, and the self-destructive. Illuminating parts of the music industry most don't talk about, this is show business without the showbiz.

Stop Requested, *stories by* Wyatt Doyle; *illus.* Stanley J. Zappa

"A series of rueful, witty and occasionally heartwrenching stories about riding the bus in LA. Doyle finds consequence in the inconsequential. He's Bukowski without the nasty streak. And he's real good. Highly recommended." —Marc Campbell, *Dangerous Minds*

---

nu luna, *a novel by* Andrew Biscontini

After 400 years of colonization, the moon is home to nearly a billion people, living in a crowded industrial police state on the verge of collapse. *nu luna* is a deeply personal matinee space adventure, spun through an improbably plausible future history. The future is beautiful and dangerous.

Dollar Halloween

Documenting off-brand junk and sparkly death totems, made to be thrown away. Where there's a need, or even a mild desire, a dollar store stands ready to fill it for whatever you've got in your pocket.

I Need Real Tuxedo and a Top Hat!

On the buses, on the corners, in the city streets. Portraits and lives of the forgotten, the avoided, the ignored. Street people and street life in raw, poignant photographs and stories.

Buty-Wave Is Now Closed Forever

Things that are gone, and things that remain. Includes portraits of Rev. Raymond Branch, Georgina Spelvin, Ray Bradbury, George Clayton Johnson, Tura Satana, Ernest Borgnine, and Carl Ballantine.

Jorge Amaya Doesn't Live Here Anymore

Abandoned places, empty spaces, forgotten faces. Indelible images from across the United States, documenting the wreckage and remnants of the American experience after the parade has passed.

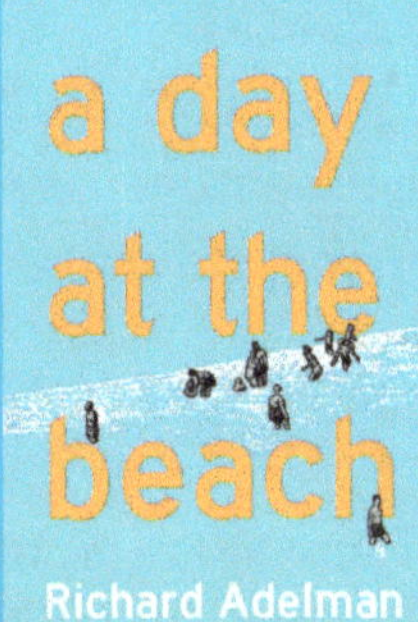

Teacher Tales, *a novel by* Richard Adelman

For 40 years, Mr. Kessler has kept his head down and not made waves. But new acquaintances and bad decisions in his final year before retirement bring his ordered world crashing down around him—tragically and hysterically. A smart and darkly comic novel.

A Day at the Beach, *a novel by* Richard Adelman

Atlantic City, summer of '63. A boy. A girl. And the other boy, who reluctantly pretends to date her to help his pal. A funny, nostalgic novel of young love, best friends, and poetry, capturing one 12-year-old's last great summer as a kid down the shore.

Nimrodia, *poems by* Eric Reymond

Visual art and ancient history are the starting point for most of the poems in this collection, as the modern world intersects with these domains again and again. Though language, culture, and time may divide us, these are also the forces that link us together.

Sub-Sub Librarian, Extracts on a, *poems by* Eric Reymond

The title poem imagines *Moby Dick*'s Sub-Sub Librarian experiencing transcendence and illumination through his wide readings. Additional poems find inspiration in texts as diverse as contemporary poetry, vocabulary quizzes, and course syllabi.

Pop's Cookie Duster
by Don & Lee Doyle; *illus.* Annette Debevec

Rainy afternoons aren't much fun for two lively little girls who love to play outside. But a hands-on kitchen activity with their visiting Pop might just save the day!

Things That Were Made for Love: The Songsheet Art of Sydney Leff
Wyatt Doyle, Hal Glatzer, Norman von Holtzendorff, *editors*

The first-ever songsheet art collection presenting the cream of the Jazz Age illustration artist's work on songsheet covers from 1924–1932. A gorgeous visual feast that playfully captures the moods, elegance, and style of an era.

#new texture Music

CD / DOWNLOAD

I've Got Heaven on My Mind
Reverend Raymond Branch

Sixty Goddammit Josh Alan

Jimmy Angelina s/t

Cursed Carolina

Continental / International
Jon E. Edwards

Map of the Moon s/t

Sing-Song Songs
Stanley J. Zappa

Free / Refuse
Hall, Skrowaczewski, Zappa

Live a Little
Manzappaczewski

The Stanley J. Zappa Quartet
**Plays for The Society
of Women Engineers**

Crossing Guards
Carter, Leffue, Sikora, Zappa

Turkey Bacon Donuts Bitches
MANZAP REBORN

Balloons

Daniel Carter,
Nick Skrowaczewski,
Stanley J. Zappa

new texture